THE SILO

MELANIE LOPATA

Book Cover by Tina Sanders

First edition 2024

Proofreading by Nadara "Nay" Merrill of Nay's Notations

ISBN: 9798218456986

Published by Get It Write Publishing Company

Many thanks to my beta readers, Tina Sanders and Niki Gregory, for taking the time to read this, giving me superb feedback, and pushing me to finish when I wanted to give up. To Nay for editing/proofreading, and Tina for final proofreading! I couldn't have done it without all of you!

For Jeff, my childhood best friend.

We had such great memories on Shells Bush Road.

(I'm glad we never climbed up the silo.)

Before…

They were singing "Ring Around the Rosie" when Jeff stopped and said, "What's a posy?"

Melissa huffed in annoyance at being interrupted. Jeff always did that; he always interrupted with one of his stupid questions. All she wanted to do was play "Ring Around the Rosie." Was that too much to ask?

"It's . . . Um, it's . . . Oh, who cares! Let's just play!"

Melissa grabbed Jeff's hands and began twirling. Her blue ruffled dress flounced around her eight-year-old body while her dark hair flew around with the movement. She laughed and pulled Jeff along while singing the silly little rhyme, all the while having no idea what a "posy" was. Jeff, however, did not need to know that she didn't know.

After several rounds of "we all fall down," and laughing gaily, Melissa became bored with the game.

"Come on," she commanded. "Let's go play in the barns!"

"Um, do you think it's ok?" Jeff asked, worried. He was a bit more cautious than Melissa but often let her boss him around. Jeff and Melissa were the same age, but Jeff was so thin—almost frail-looking—and about an inch shorter than Melissa, which made it easier for her to boss him around.

"Jeff!" Melissa yelled, her hands on her hips. "It's *fine*. Mommy said we could go in the barns if we stayed away from the animals. Oh, and we aren't allowed in the silo. Or any of them. I don't know why since there aren't any animals in those." Her parents had forbidden her and Jeff to play near the silos. Her daddy told her that if they played near the silos, they'd be tempted to go inside, and they could never, *ever* go inside. She had no idea why. Melissa didn't even know what was inside of the silos.

Jeff allowed Melissa to grab his hand, and he ran with her down the gentle slope of the backyard toward the barns. Jeff loved playing with Melissa, even if she was bossy at times. Ok, *most* of the time. They loved to read books together and build forts and play outdoors. During the school year, they would have a snack while working on homework together at Melissa's house, then they would put their play clothes on and play outside whether there was snow or sun.

"Come on, pokey!" Melissa called as she ran ahead of Jeff. Her hair danced after her as she laughed playfully, her blue eyes sparkling with joy. She loved summertime because she didn't have to go to school, which meant more time to explore the barns and the woods behind her house and build forts with her best friend, Jeff.

Jeff caught up and the two ran into the largest of the

three barns. He was starting to become excited at the thought of exploring or playing something different.

The smell of hay filled their nostrils, and the mooing of cows could be heard from the room beneath them. Melissa and Jeff ran up and down the bales of hay, laughing and playing tag. They ran downstairs to see the cows—but didn't get too close—and waved to Melissa's daddy and the farm help, who were milking cows and mucking the stalls.

After running through the barns, Melissa and Jeff went back outside to catch their breath and get away from the smell of cow manure.

"Hey, Lissy. What's that?" Jeff pointed to the silo and Melissa looked up, squinting her eyes. All she could see was the ladder that led up to the big hole in the silo.

"I don't see anything. Come on, let's build a fort."

"No . . . wait. I thought I saw a bird fly inside. A *big* one!" Jeff exclaimed excitedly.

I looked at him like he was crazy. Who cares about a bird?? I don't say that. Instead, I say, "We're not allowed in the silo, remember?"

"I thought you were the brave one," Jeff challenged as he narrowed his eyes at her.

"Oh," Melissa said. "Ok, you want to be like that?"

Jeff puffed up his chest a little, attempting to look brave.

I knew he wasn't. He was calling my bluff.

Melissa gave a wicked grin. "Fine. Let's go."

"Oh, no, I mean . . . we shouldn't," Jeff stammered, letting go of his bravery.

"Come on, chicken! You want to go, so let's go! Look, we've never been in there. We don't even know what it looks like or why the grown-ups don't want us there. So, let's check it out!"

"I was kidding, Lissy," Jeff muttered. "Let's build a fort."

"Jeff . . ." Melissa started with a sly voice. He heaved a sigh, knowing what was coming—something he could never, ever ignore. "I dare you," she said with narrowed eyes.

Jeff turned his head toward Melissa and looked her in the eyes. "Ok," he whispered.

CHAPTER 1

25 Years Later . . .

I WATCH AS the cab pulls away from the side of the road, leaving me alone in the country—basically in the middle of nowhere.

"I'm home," I whisper to no one.

Thunder rolls then, almost as if in response. Lightning flashes above, giving me glimpses of the structure before me. There's no rain, but I can sense it's coming. The air chills around me, causing me to shiver involuntarily. The light jacket I wear does nothing to keep the damp, cool air off my body.

I stare at the house while a breeze flutters around me.

Melanie Lopata

The two-story farmhouse before me stares back. Its darkened windows, damaged paint, and crooked porch roof provides little comfort. How long has it sat vacant? How long has it been since friends gathered around the table for home-cooked dinners, coffee, and dessert, the sound of laughter filling the house? I have vague memories of those things, yet the fog continues to hang over my mind like some force not wanting me to remember.

The breeze gently nudges me. One foot in front of the other; I can do this. I take a deep breath and step forward, gripping my duffel bag in one hand and a grocery bag in the other. The evening scent of country air tickles my nostrils, reminding me that I need to get in and settle before dark.

I walk down the long sidewalk that leads to the front porch and through the door. I barely make out a round plastic thing next to the door that has a switch on it. Holding my breath for good luck, I flip the switch and am relieved when dim light floods the porch. I was told that the house was kept up even after my grandmother went to a nursing home, and I am relieved.

I squint, making out some things in the dimly lit room. Junk. It's all junk. A recycling bin sits in one corner next to a small chest freezer. The other side of the porch contains a chair that looks like it has seen better days, a box full of old tools, some cardboard boxes, a pair of sneakers, and a pile of things I can't make heads nor tails of. A glance at the ceiling shows cobwebs lacing from one rafter to another, practically making a curtain on the ceiling. I let out a shudder and shake my head, reaching for the door leading to the kitchen. Unlocked. Of course. The lock is old-fashioned, and from what I remember, there was never a key—not that we had, anyway. Of course, twenty-five years ago, I guess it was ok to leave your house unlocked. Nowadays, it wouldn't be smart.

The door creaks open, and I step over the threshold. I stand in the kitchen of the old farmhouse—the house I once lived in as a child—its musty smell infiltrating my senses. Shadows appear before me and in corners, but I can still make out what remains of the kitchen. I see a string hanging over the table and pull it. The light comes on, and I set my bags down and look around, noticing a large wooden table in the middle of the room and counters with little space on them due to . . . stuff.

My parents had the farmhouse table since they were married, handed down to them from my mom's parents. I remember because I asked my mom once why they kept the old dinged-up table, and my mom told me it was special to her and my dad. God, the time I spent in this kitchen . . .

"Melissa, sit down and eat!" Mommy spoke sternly, but there was

a smile tugging at her lips. Papa sat quietly, not daring to cross Mommy, especially when she scolded me. I sat with one leg outside my chair, bouncing up and down in anticipation of finishing my meal so I could go back outside and play. I just had to get more playtime before dark!

"Who was I playing with?" I wonder aloud to the cold, empty kitchen. *Why can't I remember?* I shake my head. It doesn't matter. Though I don't remember much from my childhood at this house—on the farm—I'm confident memories will come pouring back soon enough.

Thunder rolls again, and there's another flash of lightning. I better get my meager groceries put away and try to get settled in. I brought some things from my former home, like canned food, muffins in a sealed bag *(yum . . . processed food)*, and some bottled water, but I don't want to put anything away in the cupboards since I don't know what shape they're in, or what may live there. I shudder at the thought.

I open a few drawers until I find one that holds folded towels, and I pull it out and shake it, just in case, then quickly wipe the table off and set my grocery bag on it. I peek my head in the bathroom. Other than some cobwebs—ok, *many* cobwebs—the room seems fine. I mean, it's just a bathroom: toilet, sink, closet, tub . . . basic things you'd find in a bathroom. I notice a door in the far-right corner and slowly back out of the room, knowing that door leads to the cellar. I was never allowed down there when I was a kid, but I recall peeking in the doorway and finding narrow wooden steps and darkness below. No thank you.

I feel very weary from the travel and memories poking at my mind, trying desperately to come through, and decide it's time to find my room—or any room—and get some sleep. I'm sure my room is still the same; no one but my grandma lived here after my parents moved. I'm still curious to see it after all these years.

I glance at the kitchen door, hoping that a lock will magically appear. Nope. Anyone can just walk in. I feel a little flutter of fear. I am in the middle of nowhere, after all. I bet if I had to scream, no one would even hear me! Well, nothing can be done now. Hopefully, there will be no intruders. I think my over-imaginative mind is just trying to take over my thoughts. I push them out.

I see a flashlight on the counter and test it. It works. I'll keep it on me while I make my way to my room. I grab my bag, then head to the living room, glancing around as I do. I recognize the old desk, woodstove, and recliner, but the couch and upright chair are not familiar. I'm itching to look through the desk, but tomorrow can be for exploring; it's too late in the day now, nearly bedtime. *My* bedtime, rather. I'm used to going to bed earlier than people normally do.

I ignore the door to my right, knowing it leads to what I used to call the playroom, and instead head straight to the door I know will open to a hallway with stairs going to the second floor.

The door creaks open and I walk through. The flashlight seems to be dimming, so I turn right and quickly hurry up the carpeted steps, shaking the flashlight as I do. I'm not sure if that will help—maybe rattle the batteries?—but I remember my father doing that anytime his flashlight started dimming. I climb the stairs and can feel a pull and ache in my left leg. It's always been there, but no one knows why. Doctors simply told me I had a bad sprain when I was young. Given everyone's vague answers, I never believed them. I feel like my entire life is a lie, one after another. Doctors, therapists . . . my parents.

I know the door at the top of the stairs leads to what used to be my room, so ignoring my surroundings, I open that door and step inside. Waving the dim light around, I see a room that looks like it hasn't been changed in years. There's a twin bed made up with a baby-blue comforter with a pretty flowery design on top. The bed sits between two windows with lace curtains, a dresser on one side and a nightstand on the other.

Where did my toys and stuffed animals go? Surely, I must have had many of them. Don't all kids? I shrug, deciding not to let it bother me. Maybe my parents gave them away. I wouldn't blame them.

I'm so exhausted. I just want to crawl into bed. After changing into comfy shorts and a tank top, I plop onto my bed and my mind drifts back to the days before I returned home.

"You're sure you're ready to return?"

I nodded with what I hoped was confidence and boldly declared, "Yes. Yes, I am ready."

The room was quiet for a moment before my therapist continued. "Melissa, this is a very . . . delicate situation. You're positive you're ready to return?"

"I assure you, I am ready, and I know that you know I am ready. Besides, where else am I going to go?" I paused before adding, "And I want to find out what happened to me as a child that had me removed from the only home I knew."

Dr. Hanson nodded and didn't argue. He often did that. I waited as he stroked his beard and stared at me with his big brown eyes through dark-rimmed glasses.

Finally, he said what I knew he would say. "Sometimes it is best to leave the past in the past."

I shook my head and sighed, then sat back in my chair. It was a comfy chair, one made of leather, just like the rest of the furniture in the office. Was that a staple of therapists' offices? Leather furniture? I gazed out the window, spotting birds flitting about, noticing how free they were. And here I was.

"I need to do this. Alone. Because I am *alone." I knew my grandmother was living in a nursing home with Alzheimer's and couldn't help me. And my parents . . . well, they couldn't help me either.*

Dr. Hanson nodded again. I swear he was made up of bobblehead material. He nodded a lot. "Well"—he stood up, dropping his notebook on his oversized oak desk—"I guess we're done here, Melissa. I wish you luck on this journey. Please call me if you need anything."

I stood up as well, placing my hand in my therapist's waiting hand. "I'm well enough to do this. I'm happy to be released."

"You were never kept prisoner, Melissa."

"Oh, I assure you, Dr. Hanson, I was." And with that, I walked out of the office, down the long hallway, out the front door, and into the warm day. I didn't look back.

Now I'm facing the past head-on. Tomorrow, I will explore the rest of the house, visit the barns, and try to piece my past together, for what my dreams have shown me in recent years, something happened here, and I intend to find out what.

CHAPTER 2

PACHELBEL'S "CANNON IN D" plays softly on the piano, the notes floating up and through the room. Its effortless beauty is smooth and soothing like a baby's lullaby.

"Melissa, dear, listen to Mommy play. Here, like this. It's classical. You'll love this piece. Do as Mommy does . . ."

I listened to my mommy playing the piano and wished I could be as talented as her. Right now, at my age, I can only play some starter songs. It really stinks. I want to play what Mommy is playing.

"Melissa, sweetie, listen to Mommy. Listen . . ."

My eyes flutter open. I lie there unable to move. *Where*

am I? What is that sound? What—

The music. The song . . . I don't hear it anymore. Where had that come from? Is the piano still here, in the playroom, which is below my bedroom? But that's silly; no one is in the house but me.

So who is playing?

My heart is pounding. I throw the covers over my head, feeling silly as I do but thinking they can provide me with a sense of security, and as I drift off to sleep, the faint sounds of Pachelbel's "Cannon in D" are, once again, playing.

A few hours later, I wake up to birds chirping outside my windows, sunlight streaming in. It's the end of August, so the weather isn't entirely cold yet, but there's a slight chill in the air. The rising sun casts a warm glow through the glass, creating a peaceful atmosphere.

I roll out of bed, still feeling a bit groggy due to fitful dreams, and shuffle to my duffel bag. It's the only possession I have left after leaving my former life that I know very little of. Inside the bag, I find a few basic necessities, but I will need to do some clothes shopping soon, maybe at a thrift store. The clothes I brought with me are probably outdated and no longer suitable for my new life. Maybe I can find a used clothing store nearby where I can grab the things I need. Or I can see if my mom's clothes fit me; I remember her as being around 5'2", the same height I am now. She had the same petite build. Of course, her clothes would be outdated too, but for hanging around here, they'd work. I make a mental note to check her room out later. It's not like I'll need *new* clothes. Where am I going to go?

I decide to go downstairs through the other hallway instead of the one I came through last night. The door from my room leads into a small bedroom before taking me into the hall. As I step through the bedroom, I am faced with a cluttered sight. I suppress the urge to sigh. Cluttered seems to be the theme of this house. There are boxes that look like they've seen better days, piles of clothes, and some random broken furniture nearly covering the worn red carpet. It smells musty, and I cover my nose as I hurry through to the hallway.

The hallway is more like another room—much larger than the one I just passed through. To my right is another door, which I assume leads to another bedroom. Or maybe a bathroom? I have no memory of that. I'll have to check that room out at some point. Straight ahead is a stairway, inviting me to move forward. However, the hall is full of boxes and junk, making it difficult to navigate.

Had my mother or father been hoarders? Maybe *they* weren't but Grandma was. The thought is unsettling, and I find myself questioning everyone's mental state. It's not just the clutter that catches my attention. The cobwebs hanging from the ceiling make me feel queasy. The sheer number of them is overwhelming, and their presence is disturbing. It feels like stepping back into a forgotten and neglected space. Why didn't anyone keep the house up? As I reflect on the cluttered hallway and cobweb-infested rooms, I question the habits of those who once inhabited this house. Where did everything come from? And who is responsible for the accumulation of dust and cobwebs? My grandmother lived here after I was sent away and continued to live here after my parents died; did she never clean? The questions weigh heavily on my mind, but for the time being, I will focus my efforts on cleaning and making this place my own.

In an effort to clear the cobwebs, I pick up what looks like a broken chair leg and swing it around the hall, knocking down every web in my path. The satisfaction of ridding these webs is short-lived, however, as I continue to stumble my way through the hallway.

Finally, I reach the top of the stairs, where memories try to surface. I vaguely remember these stairs from my youth, but now they seem steeper and more challenging as an adult. Nothing seems scary as a child. I am sure I used to be so carefree, never worrying about running down the stairs or climbing trees. But now . . .

With cautious steps, I descend, using the wall as a railing. Each creaking step feels unsteady beneath my weight, and I navigate through with caution. Halfway down, I stop, my ears thinking they hear whispers of voices past. Or is it the wind? My mind doesn't know anymore.

When I reach the bottom, I push open the louver door and step into the kitchen. Sunlight streams through the window, illuminating dust particles in the air. I take a moment to breathe in, feeling a sense of relief as I step into a slightly more organized space. However, the sight before me is far from pristine. Today, I will make a concerted effort to rid this room of dirt and clutter. It will be a task that requires both physical and mental effort, but I am determined to create a clean and welcoming space for myself. Who knows how long I'll be living here?

Wait . . .

Coffee. I need coffee. It's my morning ritual. I look around and don't spot a coffeemaker. I am confused. I do remember my family drinking coffee. *Sure, they hoard everything else but get rid of the coffeemaker.* Then my mind reminds me that we only used a percolator on the stove. My shoulders slump as I wonder if there is even coffee in the kitchen, and wouldn't it be stale? I shake my head in defeat.

Ok, no coffee for me today.

I grab a muffin from my meager food supply and head out the front door. The sun warms my face as I step out onto the sidewalk, and a slight breeze wisps through my hair. I stand still for a moment, breathing in the crisp country air, enjoying the silence around me.

The ground is damp from the rain last night, but it's not too muddy, thankfully. I swipe a stray hair out of my eyes and take a bite of the muffin while looking across the road. There's a house there. It looks familiar—a one-story structure with an attached garage, a picture window next to a small porch, and a massive lawn with a large maple tree—but I can't recall who used to live there. I hate that my mind has blocked so much of my past, my childhood. There wasn't enough therapy to help me remember.

I shake my head and look around my property as I finish my muffin. Part of me wishes I had a nice big breakfast instead of a muffin. Guess I need to start cooking at some point. Where I lived growing up, I usually had a bowl of cereal or oatmeal with toast for breakfast, but sometimes we'd have huge breakfasts of eggs, sausage and bacon, and pancakes. I'll definitely be adding those things to my grocery list.

The front lawn is big, spreading far to the right, where three large trees sit. I squint and notice a big square patch of grass that almost looks like it's covering something. Could there have been a swimming pool there that had been covered? I try to drum up a memory, but nothing comes. My mind is funny like that, choosing certain memories over others. I look over to a tree where a rope swing still hangs. I do remember that. My father made it. It's a simple thing, the swing, with just a rope and a board to sit on. I wonder if it is still sturdy.

As I walk toward the tree, I look at the cornfield stretching before me, their stalks standing tall. I'm amazed at the sight because it's all so peaceful; it's like nothing bad ever happened here and I never left. I'm glad my father rented out the land instead of selling it all. A solicitor told me about the money my father had saved for me so I could return. Apparently, no one other than my parents believed I'd ever come back, but here I am.

My attention is drawn to something, and I turn to glance over my left shoulder toward the backyard and barns situated at the bottom of the sloped yard. I catch myself wondering if someone has just run into the barn. I *swear* I saw someone. Intrigued, and not in the least bit scared, I begin walking toward the barns, my mind filling with memories of my father's farm. Although the landscape has changed significantly, I can still recall the bustling activity and vibrant atmosphere that used to surround these buildings. Now, they are hidden beneath a thick layer of vegetation, their windows and entrances almost completely obscured by trees and brush. Even the iconic trio of silos, once a prominent feature of the property, is now barely visible.

There are three barns: a medium-sized one to my left, the chicken coop sitting next to it. And in front of me is the main barn. It's very large, red in color as I think barns usually are, and I think the longest part must be where the cows were kept. Its paint is badly peeling, and some of the windows are broken. The main entrance has a huge gaping entrance.

As I continue my descent down the gravel path, I can't help but feel a sense of nostalgia. The barns were once a place of joy and hard work, where my father and his employees tended to the animals and cultivated the land. Now, they stand as a testament to the passage of time, a reminder of the changes that have occurred over the years. I take a deep breath of the fresh country air and close my eyes, recalling scents from my early years: fresh baled hay, newly cut grass, animals.

I near the barns, and a sense of unease begins to creep its way into my heart. The overgrown nature of the property adds an air of mystery, making it difficult to discern what might be lurking in the shadows. But for some reason, I can't shake the feeling that someone is there watching me. I'm a pretty strong woman—I'm sure I could hold my own if push came to shove—but having a weapon to help defend myself would be handy, should someone be waiting for me. But that's silly, isn't it? Of course no one else is here. My overactive imagination is once again wreaking havoc on my brain.

Despite my feelings, I press on, push aside the branches, and cautiously approach the barns. The silence around me is deafening, broken only by the rustling of the leaves and the distant sound of birds chirping. The once familiar scent of hay and manure is replaced by the earthy aroma of decay.

I step over to the wall of the barn and peer through a crack in one of the dilapidated windows, suddenly catching a glimpse of movement. Someone is inside, their figure obscured by the darkness. There *is* someone here! Or some*thing*. My heart beating fast, I take a step back, my mind racing with possibilities. Should I confront the person? Alert the authorities? Or is this just another anomaly in the abandoned space?

Pushing aside any sense of sanity, I cautiously continue my journey, walking away from the window I just looked through, my mind filled with questions and curiosity. Mother used to tell me my curiosity would get the best of me some day. What's that saying? "Curiosity killed the cat," or some such thing. I'm certainly not going inside the barn where I think I saw someone; I'm merely going to look around the property, and should that person—or thing—come out, I'll deal with it then. *Stupid, stupid girl*, I think to myself while trudging through the grass.

The large mouth of the biggest barn gapes at me, the doors wide open and looking like they're hanging from their hinges. The silo standing next to it seems enormous and foreboding. Its concrete structure looks cracked in places, the attached ladder rusted. It seems so familiar. Little feet jumping up, arms stretched, trying to reach the lowest rung to climb up.

My steps slow as trepidation snakes through my body, and I let out a shudder. I can't take another step. I'm standing in front of the barns, frozen in time—but *what* time? Memories shoot through my mind so fast I can barely catch any of them to think about it. I close my eyes and see flashes of children running across the lawn, men with overalls and big boots mucking through barns. Cows mooing, chickens squawking, a dog barking . . .

I take a deep breath and start walking, heading around the silo and to the back of the barns. No one is back here, and nothing came out of the barns, so I chalk it up to my imagination. I didn't *really* see anyone down here. I look over to the large tree standing tall, almost growing into one of the barns, slightly leaning toward the middle silo. My eyes rove up the silo and . . .

I stand still, my body refusing to move, yet inside, I am shaking. My heart is pounding, and my head throbs. My feet are rooted to the spot on the gravel driveway as I stare up at the looming structure before me. My body finally lets out an outward shiver, and I wrap my arms around my waist, even though it's not cold outside.

Tall, cracked, ominous looking. That's what the silo is now. A gigantic structure that looks eerie with shadows dancing around it.

I remember this silo. Something happened here. But what? My mind races to recall the memory that has been long pressed way down, down as far as it could really get. Locked away in a safe place, never to return to my brain. But now. . .

Something.

Happened.

Here.

". . . pocket full of posies."

"What's posies?"

"It's a . . . um, oh I don't know! You know, it's like . . . well who cares?"

"Why would you have a pocket full of them?"

"I. Don't. Know. Ring around the rosie . . ."

Voices of children singing and talking are playing in my head, and I blink a few times. *What the hell? Where did that come from?* Did I just hallucinate?

I'm done for now. Feeling shaky, I decide I can't go any further, so I head back to the house, confused at my sketchy memories and longing for a cup of coffee. I don't care if someone or something is down here; they can come and get me for all I care. I've had just about enough.

CHAPTER 3

AS I WALK up the driveway, I can't help but marvel about how quiet everything is around me. Except for the occasional car driving by and some birds chirping, I'm alone. Other than the house across the road, it's just mine and no others for at least half a mile.

"Hello there!"

I spin around at the sound of a female voice. Walking toward me are two women, maybe close to my age, with big smiles. I wave, and they walk over to me, indiscreetly looking at the house.

The taller of the two women, with long, brown hair and blue eyes, says, "We're your neighbors from up the road. I'm Rachel, and this is my sister Megan."

"Oh, hi, I'm Melissa. I just—"

The younger woman lets out a gasp, and Rachel's eyes widen.

"You're Melissa?" Rachel stammers.

My brows furrow. "Yes. This is my house."

"Melissa," Megan whispers. Rachel elbows her in the side.

"Is something wrong?" I ask.

"We used to go to school together, remember?" Rachel says tentatively.

I perk up at that, hoping these women can give more insight as to what happened so many years ago and why I was sent away. "Oh! I don't remember, but I'd love to know. You see, I was sent away—"

"We know," Megan chimes in. "You were—"

Rachel interrupts with "Well, we used to ride the school bus together, and you and I attended class together since we're the same age, but we have no idea why you were—why you left." She looks around nervously. It doesn't go unnoticed that Megan glances at her sister with confusion in her eyes. What is Rachel hiding?

I try to picture myself riding on a bus with other kids but can't seem to conjure up anything. My brows furrow at the effort; like, why can't I remember much? Years and years have passed since I've been back here, yet so many memories elude me. My parents and my counselor couldn't even pull the memories from the recesses of my brain. Like they're trapped there. I don't understand why some memories are there and others aren't.

"Were we close friends?" I ask, ignoring the throbbing in my head for trying to remember things.

Megan glances at her sister. "Um, well, not really, but your neighbor? Jeff? He was like your shadow and . . ." Her voice trails off, like she realizes she said something she shouldn't have.

"Jeff?" *Who is Jeff?*

A large truck chooses that moment to roar down the road, throwing dust our way and causing all of us to cough and wave the air to rid of the smokey dirt surrounding us. Before I can explore the subject of Jeff, Rachel places a hand on her sister's arm and backs up.

"We will leave you alone now," she says. "Nice seeing you again!"

And with that, the women hurry back up the road from where they came from, seemingly forgetting that they were taking a walk. How peculiar. If I went to school with Rachel, surely she'd know what happened before I was sent away. But just like that, she leaves, as if she doesn't want to revisit the past. I sigh and shake my head. They're gone and I'm alone. Again.

The clouds are rolling in, so I decide to clean the kitchen. I find old rags and cleaning supplies. I don't think cleaning supplies expire, so I take to wiping down the counters and cupboards. It is a daunting task, but after a while, the kitchen is usable. Thankfully, I didn't find any rodents in the cupboards—just some mouse poop.

I decide to venture into town to get some groceries. Since I don't have a car, I have to call a taxi service, but that is fine. I don't plan on getting a car anytime soon. Heck, I don't even know how to drive! I was given a prepaid cell phone with limited minutes, but I use it anyway. I haven't checked yet to see if the landline phone in my house works, but I assume it is still in service since everything else is. Doesn't matter; I have a cell phone, so I'm going to use it. Cell phones are apparently popular, but I barely know how to use the prepaid one I was given. It doesn't bother me that I'm "behind in the times." I just want a simple life.

I climb into the backseat and direct the driver, then sit back and watch the landscape as we pass. There are so many hills and cornfields up here. It's beautiful, actually, but seems far away from civilization, even though it's not. I finally lay my head back and close my eyes.

Not too long after, I open my eyes and see we're in town. The driver is heading down what looks like a main street—bars, apartment buildings, and other little businesses—and I'm disappointed to see dilapidated buildings lining the street. Sure, there's the library and post office and a few other decent-looking buildings, but the apartment buildings are falling apart and what seems like homeless people are hanging around everywhere. I left here at a young age, so I don't remember much, but it's still sad to see this town in a state of such . . . disarray.

We get to the grocery store, and I promise the driver I'll only be about ten minutes, then head inside, bustling about so I don't have to rack up cab fare. I feel eyes on me everywhere I go; people whispering. Everyone knows everyone else's business in these small towns, so I am not surprised that people are whispering about me. It also doesn't surprise me that some of the older men and women stop me in the grocery store to offer their sympathies about my parents. I am surprised that they remember *me*. I evade personal questions; I don't want people to know my business. I appreciate people asking how I am, but asking where I've been is off-limits. I'm *so* not about to tell them the truth! Though, perhaps they know the truth anyway. I've no idea who knows what around here. Thankfully, my little white lies work, and soon, they leave me alone.

I quickly grab some necessities—food, coffee,

toiletries—and even throw in a book to read by one of my favorite authors, then hurry out to the taxi to take me home. I make it back to the house just before the clouds let loose with rain. I spend time putting groceries away, and I feel happy that I've now got quite the stock of food for a while. Except for bread and things like butter and milk, I'll be set for a few weeks. I also plan on cooking and freezing meals and doing some baking—or attempting, anyway, since I don't have a lot of experience—and learning to survive on my own. I know I have money in a trust my parents set up for me, but how long can that last? I'm young; I could live another sixty plus years. I'll need to get a job at some point. Doing what, I have no idea. I'm not even sure what my skills are. Does reading books count as a skill? I don't think I can make a living doing that.

After putting the groceries away, I set about making afternoon coffee. I bought the biggest container of coffee I could find while in town and cannot wait for it to brew—well, perk, that is. I plan on curling up on my favorite old chair in the living room and starting my new book. I love reading; I always have. Maybe, I think, someday I'll write a book of my own.

I fill the percolator with water, then stare at it for a few seconds. I really don't know what I'm doing, but how hard can it be? I put the tin basket onto a stem thing, then set it in the water. Then I measure out the coffee grounds. Ok, now what? After a moment, I turn the stove on and figure it has to boil for a few minutes, then it will be done. Only one way to find out.

After turning the burner on, I look up and out the window above the sink. The cornfield is barely visible with the rain outside. I vaguely remember playing in those cornfields as a child. Memories come and go with me, always flitting about like little birds but never staying long. I used to sled in the winter and run through large corn stalks as they grew high. I was always with someone . . . that, I do know. But I can't remember who, exactly, or why I don't remember.

Something suddenly appears in my vision, and I blink twice. A figure of . . . *something* is running toward the barns. *Again?* This is getting ridiculous. I was just down there earlier. Is my imagination working overtime again or is someone really messing with me? I'm not afraid; I grew up here and know that all types of animals roam about on farms—active farms or not. But why would a person be on my property? And why wouldn't they just come to the house and ask me if they could explore instead of sneaking about?

I quickly turn the burner off and set the percolator

aside, then hurry out into the rain, my feet squishing in my flip flops as I run through the grass. I should have thrown sneakers on, but I live for bare feet or flip flops. I hate socks and sneakers. The air is chilly, but the rain is merely a drizzle now. I shouldn't be doing this; I should call the cops or 911. But alas, I do it anyway.

I head down the hill, and when I reach the bottom, I crouch behind a bush in front of the main barn and wait. I strain my ears to hear any sort of movement, but the rain on the metal roof of the barn takes over all hearing at this point.

I wait. And wait. I wrap my arms around my waist and am shivering from the cool rain. I'm soaked. Finally, I stand up, thinking how silly I am. As if an intruder would show themselves. I don't even have a weapon! What am I going to do? Fight someone with my bare hands? As I said, I can hold my own, but if someone else has a weapon, that's a different story.

Suddenly, something flies out of the broken window of the barn and heads right toward me. I scream and duck, covering my head. When I look up, all I see is something small and dark flying away. A bat? A bird?

Ugh, get ahold of yourself, Melissa!

I decide it's time to leave the barns and head back to the house to finish making coffee. I'm drenched and miserable now. At this point, I should skip the coffee and go straight for the wine! I did pick some bottles of wine up in town, and I spotted some half-empty whiskey bottles in one of the cupboards of my house. I have no idea if alcohol expires, but if worse comes to worse . . .

"Melissa," Dr. Hanson said as he looked at me over his glasses that sat perched on the tip of his nose. "I want to address something with you."

I waited. I'd learned, in years of therapy, to wait until Dr. Hanson continued, instead of getting on the defense as I was prone to do. He didn't disappoint.

"It seems you've been consuming more alcohol lately, and—"

"What?" I jumped in, not waiting for him to finish his sentence. "Who said that? We're allowed alcohol; I read the rules." It was true. The house where I was living said the residents were allowed alcohol as long as there was no destruction or public drunkenness, and if the facility managers thought there was a problem, we had to get help—or at least talk to someone about it. I did not *have a problem.*

Dr. Hanson waited a beat, then said, "Yes, you're allowed alcohol. But one of the staff have expressed some concern recently, as she's seen you coming home more often with a bag from the liquor store. I just want to know if you want to talk about it."

He waited, and I fumed. It must have been Alexandra; she's always been a snitch. However, to show my therapist I was completely fine, I took a deep breath before speaking. "I do drink a little more wine than I should"—I ignored his raised eyebrows— "But I have it under control. Besides, I recently found out my parents are dead, my grandmother is in a nursing home, barely lucid, and I'm going back to a house I haven't been in for over twenty years. Alone. Anyone in my shoes would drink a little."

There went those damn eyebrows again. He didn't speak for a moment, just nodded his head. Then he said, "Ok, Melissa. But you know I'm here if you need extra time, extra sessions."

I sat up straight and lifted my chin slightly. "I'm completely fine."

And I *am* fine. I remember my sessions with Dr. Hanson like they were yesterday. If I spoke to him today, I'd tell him I am still fine. I just like a little wine once in a while. And coffee, of course. The other residents teased me mercifully about my caffeine intake. That, I didn't mind. Addictive personality or not, I am who I am and not about to change.

As I approach my house, I glance up and notice a light shining through one of the smaller windows in the house across the road. A silhouette of a person is standing at the window, looking out at me. I cover my mouth to prevent myself from screaming and quickly run inside the house, slamming the door shut behind me. I lean against the door, breathing heavily. This is the first time I've seen any sign of life across the road since I returned, and yet there was someone at the window. I saw them. I'm not sure why I had that reaction. Probably because I didn't expect someone to be standing in the window!

Suddenly, a flash of lightning illuminates the sky outside, causing the lights to flicker. I quickly grab some flashlights and candles in case the power goes out. Against my better judgment, I peek through the small window in my kitchen facing the road and notice that the light in the house across the road has vanished, and there is no one standing at the window.

CHAPTER 4

I WRAP MY arms around my waist, shivering. I'm positively unnerved by the events of the day so far. Am I losing my mind? Again? No. I can't. I was allowed out—well, allowed to come *here*. I can't blow it. Not when I am desperate for answers and my own life. A life without caregivers, therapists, *helpers*.

Thunder crashes, and I jump as the lights flicker. Then I notice that the bathroom light is on, but I never turned it on. That's strange. Maybe I *did* turn it on and don't remember. That must be it.

I step inside the bathroom and hurriedly check behind the shower curtain to make sure no one is hiding there. All clear. I check the closet next to the tub. All clear. Then I turn and notice the door to the basement. I feel that's an odd place for an entrance to the basement to be, but that is how the farmhouse was built over a hundred years ago. There's an entrance to the basement from the side of the house, but I'm not about to go outside in a storm, especially if I find I can't open the hatch doors.

While I question why I'm about to look down there now, during a storm, curiosity triumphs over sensibility, and I turn the handle and push the door open. The light switch is to my right, so I flip that on. A very small landing is a step down, and the stairs are to my right. I carefully step onto the landing and look down. The stairs look old and don't even seem safe. But then again, I don't think they ever were. My memory eludes me, but I'm pretty sure I've been down here as a child. I must have sneaked down because my parents surely wouldn't have allowed me to go down—not by myself anyway. It doesn't seem like a finished basement, from what I can see, so I'm sure it's not entirely safe.

Even though I know how stupid it is to investigate a creepy basement during a storm, after hearing and seeing things—I should know better—I still slowly make my way down into the cold, dark space. As I go, I swat cobwebs away with my hand, trying not to scream. I hate spiders.

When I reach the bottom step, I realize this isn't a

basement; it's a *cellar.* Cold, damp, stone walls that aren't smooth, and a dirt floor. Definitely not a basement. Basements are nicer, and some of them are finished, albeit creepy in my opinion. A cellar is a cold area that isn't finished and only holds a fuse box and oil tank or water heater or whatever else houses need.

I glance around and see a large contraption, which I'm guessing is the oil tank to heat the house. There is a fuse box on the wall to the left of that. Some weird-looking rusty objects are strewn around. There are some rickety-looking shelves along one part of the wall. I don't investigate because it looks like a breeding ground for spiders and their webs.

There are a lot of shadowy areas where anything could be hiding. A shiver of fear tickles my belly. I then realize there isn't a wall in the area behind the stairs. I cautiously approach and squint through the near darkness. There are small stone stairs that lead up! It looks like there are only a handful, and they're not steep. They must lead to the exterior cellar door. I wonder whether it's locked.

I am thinking about whether I should go up the steps and try the door, but again, I worry about spiderwebs. Maybe I'll check it out when I have more light and a mask or something to shield me from anything gross.

Suddenly, the lights go out, and I hear a door slam. I

freeze where I'm standing, my heart racing. Footsteps sound above me for a few seconds and then another slam—the front door to the kitchen? There must be someone in my house!

I reach out, hoping to grab onto the stairs but instead come across something sticky—a cobweb, I think—and let out a yelp. I quickly place my hand over my mouth to muffle the sound and gag, because now I have cobwebs in my mouth. I swipe at my body and shake my head in case any spiders found there way onto my body and suppress a scream.

I stumble to the stairs and start to climb but think better of it. If the intruder closed the door, wouldn't he or she be waiting for me upstairs? Or maybe they were leaving. Why would they slam the door if they were coming in? That obviously would alert someone in the house that someone just came in. But, if I try the door to the outside, the intruder could be waiting there, expecting me to try that way. What in the world am I going to do? Why didn't I bring a flashlight down here? I want to yell—whether in fear or frustration, I don't know, but I know I can't. I must keep quiet.

I decide I have to go back up the way I came. It's the smart thing to do. I think. Taking a deep breath, I climb the stairs slowly. Upon reaching the top and running my hand against the wall so I don't fall, I suddenly feel something. It's like some sort of tool! I pick it up in case I need to use it as a weapon and turn the doorknob, then slowly push the door to the bathroom open.

Rain is pounding against the windows, and I'm suddenly weary. I'm tired of the house, of the things I've been seeing, and still not having any memory of why I left in the first place. I quickly check the kitchen and front porch, and decide if there was an intruder, they're gone now. Maybe someone was lost and didn't want to be stuck in the rain. Suddenly, my mind doesn't care anymore. If I'm going to be murdered, just let it happen already. I'm tired. I slam the door and stand in the kitchen and let out a scream of frustration. It's not fair! Why are things creepy around here?

After my outburst, I let out a huff and walk out of the room. Cold and miserable, I venture upstairs to change into comfortable lounge clothing. I stop, however, at the top of the stairs, remembering that I have very little clothes with me and none are really lounge clothes except for my pajamas. I head down the hall from my room to my parents' room instead. I open the door and see everything as it used to be, from what I can recall. There are two nightstands, one on either side of the bed, a couple of large dressers, and a wardrobe. I peek in the wardrobe, part of me fearing someone is going to jump out at me, and am shocked to see clothes still hanging there. Jewelry and watches still sit on the dressers. I would have expected their belongings to be boxed up. Instead, it's as if they still live here. I guess it's up to me to take care of it all.

I open my mother's dresser and pull out a sweatshirt and pants. I bring the clothing to my face and breathe in. Of course there's no distinct scent after all of these years, but I tear up, nonetheless. I sit on my parents' bed and stare off into space, the memory of their faces flying through my mind so fast I barely recognize them. I miss my mom and dad. I hardly saw them growing up, and now they're gone forever.

I take a deep breath and change into her clothes, putting my sorrow behind me for now. They fit well, just a little big, but it does the job. I turn off the light and head downstairs. Enough remembering. Or not remembering.

I pull a bottle of wine out of the fridge and pour myself a generous glass, coffee long forgotten, then I take it into the living room, plop down on the old, worn-out recliner, and lean my head back. Except for the sound of the rain pattering against the windows, everything is still. What am I doing here? So many lost years. Did I really think I could move back and live like everything is normal?

I take a drink of wine, enjoying the sensation of it entering my system. I don't care what they thought of me at the home; I don't have a problem with alcohol. It relaxes me. And right now, I need it.

After another sip of the refreshing wine, I take a deep breath and start to think about what I *do* know. I know I lived here for the first eight years of my life. I have vague memories of my childhood, but at certain times . . . well, nothing. One day, as a kid, I woke up in a room in some weird place—not a hospital, really, but there were doctors and nurses. They tried to explain to me that I had been asleep for almost a month. A month! My little child brain couldn't fathom that (Heaven forbid they call it what it was—a coma), and my parents didn't speak much of it. All I knew is that my parents were very excited that I wasn't sleeping anymore.

Several weeks later, after a lot of therapy, I came back to this house with my parents. That part, I have no memory of, but my mom told me as much. Apparently, I had nightmares every night and barely spoke, but when I did, I was incoherent. I refused to go outside. My parents didn't know why; I couldn't tell them. My mom told me the first time I rounded the corner of the house and saw the barns, I began to scream and then cried for nearly an hour until I fell asleep.

When it was clear I couldn't stay here, my parents moved me into a beautiful, old Victorian home with many therapists—some physical and one mental—as well as ten other occupants in addition to staff. Some called it a "facility" and some "respite home." I spent the rest of my life there up until now. I can't say those were terrible years; I made some friends. I learned how to cook simple meals, though I never truly caught on, and how to do basic household chores. I learned how to use a landline phone and a computer. And, of course, I saw my therapist, Dr. Hanson, three times a week.

I think the worse part was that I was basically raised by people other than my parents and grandma. My parents lived at the farmhouse, which is several hours away from my "home," so I mostly talked to them on the phone or by letters. They visited once a month and on special occasions like Christmas and my birthday. I often wondered, during those years, if they were avoiding me. Had I done something wrong? I was just a child. I felt they had abandoned me. I still feel that way sometimes. Put in a home as a child, without knowing why, then not having my parents around! Then one day, my mother visited me and told me that my father had had a heart attack and was gone. I was an adult; I knew what "gone" meant. It hurt so much, especially because I felt my time with him was short-lived. Mom never came back after that. She died a few months later. I heard whispers that she died of a broken heart, but I never asked. It didn't matter. They weren't around anymore, and my grandma was too old to visit.

I swallow the rest of my wine to shake off the sad memories and get up to refill my glass, padding across the worn green carpet and heading into the kitchen. I shouldn't have any more, but I feel relaxed finally.

Thunder is rumbling softly, and lightning brightens the room, causing the lights to flicker. I hurry to fill my glass and get back to the recliner to try and relax. No more thinking. That does no good. Tomorrow, I decide, I'll explore the rest of the house and try to find some answers to what happened to me when I was a child. There must be clues around here. A journal. Paperwork of . . . some sort. What, I have no clue. I have no idea what I'm looking for. That's the frustrating part.

A *tap-tap-tap* on the living room window causes me to jump a little, so I hurry over and draw the curtains closed. I glance at the woodstove in the corner, wondering if it will be safe to use at some point. I hear the tapping again, and I jump again. It seems more persistent now.

That's it. I'm calling the cops.

CHAPTER 5

"SO YOU THINK you saw someone down by the barns, and this evening you heard tapping on your window. That correct?"

Officer Monroe seems to be staring me down. I nod, unable to speak. His presence isn't comforting; it's intimidating. He must be at least six feet tall, with an Army-style haircut, and muscles bigger than I've ever seen on any man. He wears a frown, possibly permanent, with steely gray eyes.

"We checked the grounds, Ms. Turner. We didn't find anything or anyone. You sure you saw something? Heard something? It's pretty deserted out here in the country. You, being a young woman and living alone, and well, maybe you're spooked. Or, perhaps . . ." He glances at the empty wine glass on the table. Oh, the nerve!

I'm seething now. He is indicating that because I am a single, young woman who lives on her own, I am helpless. I am hardly helpless. I just don't like people lurking around my property. He is also indicating that I've drunk too much. Basically, he thinks I'm wasting his time. I've seen movies; I read books. I know how this works.

"I know what I saw and heard. I also did not call you when I saw something earlier. I went down to the barns myself." I'm trying to remain calm, but it's nearly impossible because of the way this man is looking at me.

The kitchen door opens, and another officer walks in, this one shorter and stick thin. I definitely could take him down. How is he even a cop? He glances at me, then at the other officer. It doesn't escape my notice that they both slightly nod at each other—some sort of secret police code? Then the shorter one speaks.

"We didn't find anything. Everything is clear. Just call us if you, um, if you see anything."

I notice he doesn't say "If you *hear* anything." I get it. I'm wasting their time.

As they're walking out, the taller cop turns and says, "You should get a lock for this door."

I nod and close the door firmly behind them. I watch

through the living room window as they drive off, and I swear the older cop is laughing as they leave.

Feeling pretty pissed and annoyed at "the system," I grab another glass of wine and curl up on the couch. This time, however, I have a metal baseball bat next to me. Just in case. Helpless woman, my ass.

I am too wound up to sit and relax, so I decide to explore more of the house before night comes. I'm smart this time—well, not smart enough to leave this for the morning when it's light outside and I have a clear mind—and grab a flashlight to take with me . . . just in case.

The living room, laundry room, and bathroom can be reached from the kitchen. There's also a door next to the bathroom door that opens to a steep staircase that leads to the second floor from this end of the house. I poke my head into the laundry room first. Nothing exciting. A washer, dryer, drying rack, a rack holding coats for all seasons, some shelves holding odds and ends (junk, it seems), and several piles of clothes. It's odd that no one put the clothes away. They just left them in piles in the laundry room. I shake my head and go back into the kitchen, pulling the door closed behind me. I don't want to see that junk.

I go to the playroom next. An old couch and a scuffed piano sit against the wall to my left. I remember my mother teaching me to play on that old thing. In front of me is the door to the outside back patio and a pile of toys, and the rest of the room is filled with bookshelves full of what looks like puzzles, games, coloring books, and small toys. The room is something I do remember. And it has stayed the same from what my memory can drum up. It's exactly how I remember it all those years ago. How strange. It's like my parents preserved the house like a museum. I know Gram lived here, but wouldn't my parents have cleaned it out after I left? It would have made it easier for Gram to get around if there was clear space for walking.

I walk over to the couch and run my hand over the flower-patterned cloth, rough under my fingers. How many times as a child did I sit on this very couch with my mother, reading books or telling stories from our heads? Someone else sat here with me. But I have no idea who. To my left is a door, which I assume is a closet, and a doorway with no door, just a tall cabinet. I smile, remembering that my dad used to keep records and encyclopedias in there. I also used to climb on top of it and sneak to the stairs to get up to my room or to get from the stairs to the playroom and outside if I wanted to avoid being seen.

"Wait for me, Melissa! WAIT!"

I ignored the cries; he was such a baby. He should keep up. We were, after all, playing "spies" and we couldn't be caught.

"Come on, slowpoke!" I yelled, then I hopped effortlessly onto the edge of the stairs, grabbing hold of the railing and sliding through the missing rails to get to "safe" on the stairs.

One of my favorite things was sneaking in and out of the playroom this way. I don't think my parents know I do this. I love having this secret.

A clap of thunder snaps me out of my memories. I remember playing that game; I remember—

Thunder again, louder this time, with lightning following. Why does it storm so much here? The lights flicker and then go out. My heart jumps, and I spin around to head out of the room when I see someone standing outside in the rain on the other side of the window.

I scream and cover my eyes. I try to take deep breaths, and finally, when I open my eyes, there is no one in the window—no one in the room with me. The police said they didn't find anyone. But there were only two of them. Did they really look well enough? Murderers are good at hiding.

I take more deep breaths before hurrying out of the room. I don't even bother to turn my flashlight on, which is stupid because I'm tripping over crap that's in my way. Doesn't matter, though. I know the way. I hurry to the kitchen, gasping for air as I go, and, once again, shove a chair under the door handle to keep anyone from coming in. Stupid house. Stupid old house with easy access to get inside and no lock on the damn door!

I grab a cold bottle of water from the fridge and practically run upstairs to my bedroom and crawl under the covers. The feel of my comforter over my body gives me a false sense of security. I feel safe. For now.

CHAPTER 6

I WAKE TO birds singing outside. Sunlight fills my bedroom, and I stretch and yawn, taking in the sights of the space I inhabited when I was a child. I desperately try to drum up some memories—a favorite doll or stuffed animal, a rocking chair, perhaps—but nothing comes. I lay there for a few minutes, thinking about the house.

Despite the exciting and nerve-racking events of yesterday, I'm feeling a little lonely this morning. After moving into the house where I ended up staying until I returned here, I grew up with many people living under one roof. We had our privacy, sure, but there was always someone when I wanted to talk or even take a walk with. Here, though, it's too quiet. Of course I have the birds outside chirping away, and I have neighbors on this road, but here in this house . . . well, I'm alone. I thought I'd be fine being alone, but I don't think I am. Do I have a choice, though?

With a sigh, I climb out of bed and dress, then head to the kitchen for coffee. I don't bother thinking about my secondhand wardrobe that I brought with me, or the fact that I can wear some of my mother's clothes; I guess I just don't care much. Besides, this house needs so much work, wearing something nice would be foolish.

I set the coffee to perk (I think I'm finally getting the hang of it), pull a blueberry muffin out of the plastic container, and sit down. I'm not hungry, really, but I know I must eat. I mull over things that have happened since I arrived, the supposed figure of someone or something down in the barn, the noises. I can't make heads or tails of any of it, so I chalk it up to my imagination and the fact that I have been known to see and hear things. I thought I moved past that, but apparently not. Well, if the police won't help me, I'm truly on my own.

I eat my muffin and drink two cups of coffee before slipping my feet into boots, then I head outside. I stand there momentarily, breathing in the fresh air of the countryside. Despite being alone, it sure is peaceful up here. A lawn mower and a tractor can be heard in the distance along with kids calling out to each other and laughing—summer sounds. I smile and walk over to a porch on the other end of the house that, I think, was the *original* house before the addition—still two stories but narrower. Funny how my brain remembers specific facts about this house, but other memories are spotty.

I step onto the porch carefully, as the two wooden steps are rotted. Junk is piled on the porch, mostly old lawn chairs and tools I cannot identify. In the corner, I spot a weed wacker. Perfect. That's what I need. In the months before returning home, I did my research on caring for a property and what tools to use, and one thing was keeping the lawn mowed and the weeds . . . well, wacked.

I step off the porch and walk to the back of the house to cut down the pesky weeds that are overtaking the back porch. My mother used to hang clothes out back; I know that because there is a clothesline hanging and a basket of wooden pins on the porch.

After looking it over and deciding it looks pretty easy to use, I pull the cord. Noting happens. Damn! Why isn't it working? I turn it over and study it, checking it out from every angle. Ahh, it's got a battery. I pry the old thing off, wondering how I can charge it or if I need to go to town to get a new one. Then I remember the junk on the front porch and head over to look through it. After about ten minutes of sifting through old tools, empty paint cans and coffee cans, and seeing a lot of dead bugs—Gross. Me. Out.—I see something that looks like a battery charger. I take it into the house, plug it in, and wala! It works. Now I just have to wait for it to charge.

After straightening out the porch a little, I'm impatient to get started with outdoor work, so I unplug the battery and take it outside to see if I can get a little juice out of the weed wacker. Thankfully, after putting the battery in and turning it on, the weed wacker roars to life. For the next twenty minutes, I successfully get rid of the overgrowth, and the area starts to look nice again.

When I'm satisfied with my work, I turn the machine off and wipe my brow. It is then that I notice the sky darkening again. "Oh no," I mutter to no one but the trees and the barns at the bottom of the yard. "Not rain again." Good old upstate New York. Heaving a sigh, I pick up the weed wacker and head back to the front to put it away and get inside before the clouds open up.

Suddenly, movement catches my eye, and I whip my head around in the direction of the barns. There's no one there. But the barns stand tall and ominous—the insides dark and branches from nearby trees slightly swaying.

Thunder gently rolls in the distance, and I set the weed

wacker down, slowly walking down the hill to the barns I so want to avoid yet want to explore at the same time. Why am I drawn to them? Is something—or someone—pulling me to them?

The wind picks up, and I shiver. I'm only dressed in jeans and a T-shirt, but even the end of summer should still hold some heat. Not in New York State, apparently.

I reach the smaller of the four barns and stand in front of the door, which is slightly ajar, and peek my head in. This was the chicken coop. I've seen pictures online and in books about farms, so I'm familiar with this smaller barn. To my left are stairs leading up to a second floor. Maybe that's where things were stored. I'm not sure. I push the door open wide and step all the way inside, an array of scents filling my nostrils—old hay and dirt. It's musty in here, and except for some crates and wood lying on the dirt floor, the room is empty. I stand there for a moment, not hearing anything. It's eerily quiet here.

Something creaks above my head, and I look toward the stairs. Should I go up? What if . . . What if someone is up there? Or an animal? Well, I didn't come this far to chicken out (no pun intended).

I slowly climb the stairs, each one creaking under my feet and wobbling just enough to make me nervous. I keep looking behind, paranoid that someone is going to sneak up on me. I've always been like that. No idea why.

When I reach the top, I turn and look at the room. To my relief, it's empty but for a few odds and ends—empty cans, jars, and broken tools—and a large wooden trunk that looks like it went through a train wreck, rusty hinges and a hook near the lid. I carefully walk over the floor and reach the trunk, kneel, and reach for the latch to open it.

"Ready or not, here I come!"

I giggled and lowered the top of the trunk while crouching down. He'll never find me here! I am so clever. I heard him outside calling my name; I heard the door creak open to the chicken coop. He looked all over. He'll never find me!

A screeching sound jolts me out of the memory, and I pull my hand away from the trunk. What was that sound? I stand quickly and look around, then carefully step forward to the only window up here. It's small and square, but there's no glass. I put my head through and look around the back yard and at the other barns but don't see or hear anything. How strange. I could have sworn I heard something.

I pull my head back in, bumping it on the side of the window slightly. The memory I just had seeps back into my mind, and I look down at the trunk near my feet. Had I hidden in this trunk as a child? Who had I been playing with? Maybe the boy who Rachel said I was friends with. Jeff? I shake my head, not remembering, then reach for the lid again, this time lifting it up and peeking inside. A small, dust-covered doll lies in the corner. I slowly reach for it . . .

"Let's play hide and seek with her!"

"NO! She'll get dirty. She'll be scared."

"Oh come on . . ."

I blink several times at the flash of a memory. It literally sounded like kids were in the room with me. This doll . . . It is small, maybe about ten to twelve inches long, with wide eyes and a bald head. It's dirty and scuffed, definitely has seen better days. The body is soft but seems like real skin, which freaks me out. It seems a little familiar, yet . . .

A flash of lightning followed by more thunder urges me to my feet, and I quickly hurry down the stairs and out the door, still holding the doll. I turn to take another look at the small barn while cradling the doll, then hurry up the hill to the house.

I run to the front of the house as the rain begins pelting my body, and when I round the corner, I skid to a stop and scream when I see someone standing there.

CHAPTER 7

"WHOA. HEY, I didn't mean to—"

"Who are you?" I take a step back from this stranger, my heart racing.

A man, taller than me, wearing jeans and a long-sleeve tee, backs up and raises his hands in surrender.

"I'm your neighbor." I slowly look to the house across the road, and he continues. "I just moved in. I knocked on your door to introduce myself, but you didn't answer, so I was about to head back home when I heard a scream."

"A . . . Wait, *I* just screamed now."

He shakes his head. "No, I heard a scream a few minutes ago. It wasn't you. It sounded like . . . well, it sounded like a little kid. Do you have—"

I shake my head, gripping the doll closer to my chest. I must look like a lunatic. "No. No kids. I didn't hear . . ."

He smiles and folds his arms over his chest. It's then that I realize the rain is still coming down, so I motion to the house, and he follows me inside. Of course I just invited a complete stranger into my house, during a storm no less. Well, I never claimed to have street smarts. I turn the light on in the kitchen and set the doll on the table, then turn to the stranger. Er, my neighbor. He's simply standing there, staring at me.

"Who are you?" I ask, wrapping my arms around my body.

"Oh, sorry. My name is Sam."

I stare at him longer than I probably should, but I'm surprised because since I've been back, there hasn't been anyone across the road. Now this guy just appears. I'm a little weirded out. Of course, finding the doll didn't help.

Get a grip, I tell myself. He's just a nice guy who moved in a cross the road. I swear I read too many murder mysteries. Taking a deep breath, I turn back to Sam and force a smile.

"My name is Melissa. I just came back . . . here . . . uh, home, er . . ." *What an idiot! Haven't you been around people before?* "Do you want . . . Would you like some coffee?" *Isn't that what neighbors do? Offer coffee? To a complete stranger?*

"I'd love some. I haven't yet unpacked, so I have no idea where the coffee pot might be." Sam laughs.

I smile and set about grabbing mugs from the cupboard—checking first to make sure they're not dusty—and pull creamer out of the fridge. Once our coffee is poured, we sit at the table and that's when I really study him. He seems to be around my age. He's definitely fit, his muscles pushing through his shirt, and his smile is charming. He's kind of handsome, even. His eyes, though. His dark eyes seem to look deep into my soul, yet they're almost empty, if that makes sense.

I pour the coffee and we sit. Sam takes a sip of his coffee without putting sugar or cream. *Yuck*. I force myself to not make a face. Not everyone likes cream and sugar; I must remember that.

"This is a nice farmhouse," Sam comments, setting his mug down on the wooden table. He runs a hand through his dark, wet hair. "You say you used to live here?"

"What?" I'm startled for a moment. "I didn't—"

"Oh, my mistake. You said 'home,' so I assumed you used to live here." He sips on his coffee and looks around. He seems very interested in the kitchen. Or maybe it's my imagination. I'm not what you'd call a social person; in fact, I haven't been around a lot of people basically my entire life. Only the people I lived with growing up, but other than that, no social interaction. I never even went to school after I came out of the coma. At the "home" where I was moved into, I had a tutor. Some would call it home-schooling.

"Yes, I grew up here. Well, I lived here until I was eight."

I drink my coffee nervously. Sam seems nice, but he *is* a stranger. And there's a storm outside. Read enough murder mysteries and you'll know how ominous the setting is. Ironic, I have no problem running down to the barns when I think I see someone, yet I feel nervous sitting in front of an actual human being. I almost chuckle at the thought.

Sam nods. "Are you glad to be back? Seems awfully large for a young woman to handle on her own."

I stare at Sam for a moment. "I'm fine. I don't even know how long I'll stay. I just . . ." I can't finish. I don't want to give this man any more information than necessary.

"I get it. I bought the house across the road, and it's great and all, but I don't know how long I'll stay."

"Well why did you move here? I mean, if you're not sure you'll stay, why buy a house?"

Sam shrugs. "Work. I have work to do, and this seems like a quiet, quaint place to do it."

I get it. We're up in the country, basically the middle of

nowhere, but town is only about a ten-minute drive, and it *is* small and quaint. There's not much there anymore; the town is basically going to pot as most small towns do. No matter how hard people try, some towns just seem not to be able to grow.

I wonder what kind of work he does, but he doesn't offer any more information, so I don't ask. His eyes land on the doll, still lying on the table. I chuckle, a little embarrassed.

"I found her—um, *it*—in the barn."

He raises his eyebrows. "Yours?"

I shrug. "I'm guessing. I mean, when I was a kid."

Sam doesn't speak, only stares at the doll. His eyes narrow, and as he brings his coffee mug to his lips, I hear him whisper, "Kristi."

"What?"

"Huh?" He sets the mug down and looks innocently at me.

"Kristi. Where did you hear that name from?"

Sam laughs. "Oh, I'm sorry. My cousin had a doll similar to yours. Her name was Kristi." He stands up suddenly and walks over to the sink, then gently places his mug inside. "Thank you, Melissa, for the coffee."

"Sure, not a problem. Sorry I didn't have anything to go

with it. I haven't had time to bake."

"No worries. You know, my mother used to make an amazing cookie called snickerdoodles. I should make them sometime and bring you a batch."

A sharp pain slices through my head, and a flash of light streaks past my eyes.

"Lissy, Lissy! Mama made us snickerdoodles!!"

"Yes! Let's bring them to our fort."

"Are you ok?"

I squint my eyes and see Sam standing over me. Where am I? I realize I am sitting at the kitchen table, and Sam is looking at me very concerned.

"Oh, I'm fine. Just had a flashback." I chuckle a little, trying to make light of it all.

"Well, take care."

I watch as Sam walks out, feeling both nervous and curious. What is so familiar about that man?

* * * * *

The sun is starting to dip behind the horizon, and I step outside with bare feet. The rain stopped not long ago, so the grass is still wet, but everything is still. The country air smells so good—fresh and like rain. I take a deep breath as I walk over the cool grass to the swing.

After pulling on the rope and adjusting the wooden seat,

I'm satisfied that it can hold my weight. I lower myself onto the swing and grip the coarse handles before pushing myself feet. With my eyes closed, I swing back and forth, the breeze whishing through my hair. I start to pump my legs and go faster, higher. A smile lights up my face as I swing, and I feel wonderful—so free.

"Time for supper, Melissa!"

I was swinging high and didn't want to stop yet, but Mommy was calling me. Just a few minutes longer. That's all I wanted, though I didn't say it out loud or Mommy would get mad.

"Two minutes," she said in her stern voice.

I knew she went inside then, so I continued to swing, higher and higher, loving the way the air felt whooshing over my body, loving the feel of freedom. Like a bird, high in the sky.

With my eyes still closed, I let myself slow down, knowing I had to go inside. When I slowed, I opened my eyes, preparing to jump off the swing.

He was standing there, staring at me, and I screamed.

"You scared me to death!" I cried out, stumbling off the swing. I had to catch myself from falling to my knees, and my hands ground in the hard dirt, causing pain to shoot through them. That made me mad.

I took a few steps toward him and slapped his arm. "What the heck?"

"I saw you swinging and wanted a turn, but then your mom called you in."

"Oh." I smooth my dress down, feeling myself calm a little.

"Be careful, Lissy. You really shouldn't go that high. You could fall and get hurt."

"I'm fine," I retorted. He was just jealous because he was too afraid to swing that high. "Come on. Let's see if you can stay for supper."

My eyes fly open with a memory and I nearly fall off the swing. I quickly plant my feet and skid to a stop, my heart thudding in my chest, my body shaking and barely able to hold onto the handles. I look up and gasp.

Standing in front of me is Sam. He's just staring at me. No smile. No frown. His eyes vacant. Just . . . staring.

I get to my feet a little unsteadily and walk toward him.

"Sam?" I whisper. It's like he's in a trance.

Then he blinks. "Oh. Hello."

"Sam, are you ok?"

"You looked so carefree. Just swinging. Not a care in the world."

"Um, ok." I back up a little, wondering if something is wrong with him.

Sam doesn't say anything else; he just starts walking away toward his house. I'm standing there, puzzled, when he turns around suddenly.

"You really shouldn't go that high. You could fall and get hurt." Then he turns and heads across the street.

My eyes widen when he says that. Those words . . . they're so familiar.

What. The. Hell.

CHAPTER 8

THE NEXT DAY, I wake early, which is a miracle since I hadn't gotten much sleep. I tossed and turned for a long time when I went to bed last night, thinking back on the day—Sam's odd behavior, the doll I found, the swing, the memories. It's all so disturbing. I have to keep a sound mind, though. I must stay on track and remember to move forward even as I regain memories of the past. I don't want to come undone. That would set me back. I don't want to go back. I am glad, however, that my memories from childhood are trying to poke through. I'll be able to piece things together soon, I think. If only I could talk to more people in this area who would have known me and my parents back then.

Putting that to the back of my mind for now, I dress and hurry to the kitchen, make coffee and some toast, and before I know it, I'm ready to tackle some chores. One of these days, I think, I'll sit and eat a proper breakfast instead of always hurrying through.

I grab a box from the front porch to start filling it with things to get rid of or donate. I begin with my mother's bookshelf—I'm assuming it's hers, as I don't think my father ever had time to read except his magazines and farming books—and once the box is full, I set that aside and walk over to the woodstove. It's definitely old, rusted in some spots, but when I peek inside, there are hardly any ashes, and it seems clean. If I can find some old wood in one of the barns, this woodstove will be handy for cold days when I don't want to use the heat. Then again, I should have someone look at it first. I don't know how long it has sat unused, and I think you are supposed to have the chimney cleaned before using a woodstove. Gosh—all the crap I need to learn as an adult on my own seems daunting.

I'm standing at the sink, washing my hands, when I have an idea. I will walk up the road and see if I can find out where Rachel and Megan live. Maybe they're sitting on a porch or working on the lawn, and I can talk with one of them. If Rachel and I went to school together, she'll certainly have memories of my childhood and why I left—or was taken away. I don't know why that's important to me, but for some reason it is. I left the "home" I grew up in, went through many, many years of therapy, and still don't know hardly a thing about my past. If I'm going to stay here, I want to know what happened.

After putting on my old sneakers and tying a hoodie around my waist, I stroll up the road past old farmhouses and some newer ranch-style homes. Some kids play in their yards, and dogs run around barking. It's a beautiful late summer day, and I'm happy to see people spending time outside. As I walk, I'm studying the houses, hoping something will click. Like, did I know anyone who lived there? Maybe kids who I played with? But nothing comes.

I slow when I approach a two-story house on my left that looks in need of repairs, but the landscaping is gorgeous. Large maple trees dot the yard, brightly colored flowers line flower boxes on windowsills next to the front door, and flower beds surround the small porch.

As I'm staring at the house, the door opens, and a child, maybe four of five, runs out, the door slamming behind her. She stops when she sees me and gives me a big, toothy grin. I stare because the girl looks exactly like Rachel. Her brown hair is short and messy, and she wears mismatched clothes like she dressed herself, but she looks happy.

"Hi!" the little girl calls out.

Before I can open my mouth, the door opens and a woman hurries out, grabbing the little girl by the hand. She looks up.

Rachel.

As soon as our eyes meet, her eyes flash with something I can't quite read, but she recovers quickly. After whispering to the girl, who then runs inside shouting something unintelligible to someone, she turns to face me and wipes her hands on her jeans.

"Hi, Melissa! What are you doing here?"

I ignore the question and walk up to the porch. Rachel steps aside and motions me to the chairs. She pulls her cardigan closer as if out of nervous habit. She's not the warmest person I've met, but maybe I'm simply more of a stranger and that makes her uncomfortable.

"Hey, Rachel. Sorry to just drop by." I sit on one of the wicker chairs (I hate whicker) and nervously tap my foot.

"Oh, it's fine. Anytime, Melissa. Um, do you want coffee, or . . ." She sits next to me.

"No, thank you. I just . . . um, I wanted to say hello and chat a bit. You know, we went to school together and all."

She nods and seems to relax a little. I can hear voices inside—small voices, those of children—and wonder if I came at a bad time. How many kids does she have in there?

"So, this is where you live," I say somewhat stupidly. Of course this is where she lives. *Ugh. Why am I so awkward with small talk?* "I mean—"

Rachel chuckles a little. "Grew up here; never left. Met my husband in high school, married after graduation."

"Oh nice!"

"Yes," she says, staring off at . . . well, nothing, really.

I wait, wondering if there's more. She doesn't say anything for a minute, so I decide to break the silence.

"And Megan?" I glance around. "Is she . . ."

"Oh!" Rachel seems to perk up at the mention of her sister. "She lives just up the road! She has an adorable little trailer. I'm glad she's close. She's the best babysitter for my kids." Rachel chuckles.

She talks about her kids for a few minutes, but I think Rachel feels a bit like I do. Edgy. Tense. *Something.*

"How are things at the house, Melissa?" Rachel asks softly. "Are you settling in? I expect it's strange being back after all these years."

"It is. I'll admit it gets a little lonely there, but I'm trying to keep myself busy." Then a thought occurs to me. I'll broach the subject of possibly seeing someone on the property. Maybe Rachel can shed some light on it. "I have caught glimpses of someone running down toward the barns. I can't seem to catch anyone when I look." I shrug and glance down, now embarrassed that I mentioned it at all.

Rachel nods. "Some people joke that your house is haunted."

I laugh at that. It's not that I don't believe in spirits and such, but I hardly think *my* house is haunted. "Well, I don't know about haunted, but I'm pretty sure someone is lurking about."

"I hope not, for your sake. This entire road, though, has history. Some of the older homes are known to hold . . . spirits."

I smile, then remember the reason I'm here. "Rachel, I grew up with people who can't tell me anything about my childhood. What happened?"

"Look, Melissa, I only remember riding the school bus with you and hanging out sometimes during recess, but that's all. One day, you were there, the next . . . well, you were gone! They say you had an accident."

"Yeah, I know that. But I was never told what the accident was. I was in a coma for almost a month!"

Rachel's eyes widen and she covers her mouth. "I'm so sorry. I had no idea. I just thought you moved. I didn't know it had been that serious."

I shrug. Strange that her parents wouldn't have heard how serious. But I don't say that. "Of course you didn't know. Seems this town is nothing but rumors and no truth."

I stand up and start pacing the porch, the children's voices inside Rachel's house becoming louder, almost drowning out my thoughts. "I just wish I had the truth. Then I can move on. There's so much I haven't been told. So much mystery surrounding my childhood and that house."

"I'm sorry I can't help. We were young when you left! No one told us anything. I mean . . ." She trails off. I know she's hiding something. She knows *something*. The first time I saw her after returning here, she had mentioned someone named Jeff.

"Rachel . . ." I start. She turns to me, and I just blurt it out. "Can you tell me about Jeff?"

Suddenly, a crash and a cry come from inside and Rachel jumps to her feet. "I have to go. I'm so sorry! Look, let's talk soon, ok?"

And just like that, I'm on the porch alone.

I stand there for a minute, half listening to the chaos inside the house while looking at my surroundings—a few houses on each side of the road, spread out enough for some privacy, fields, some cows and barns, but mostly trees—and wonder where Megan's trailer is. For a moment,

I wonder if it would be a good idea to try to find it—maybe try to get information from Megan—but decide against it. If Rachel won't tell me anything, I am sure Megan won't. And I know they know more than they are telling me. *Why does everything have to be a secret?*

With a sigh, I stand up and start walking back to my house, leaving the shouting and laughter of kids behind me. The clouds are covering the sun now, which makes it gloomy, and it matches my mood. I am no closer to finding out what happened when I was a child or who Jeff was. I feel alone. Lost. Maybe I should let it be.

As I walk, the breeze picks up, and I look at the field to my right, the corn stalks swaying slightly under the cloudy sky. Beyond the stalks, I can spot the top of two silos, and I shiver a bit.

I reach my house and glance over at Sam's. It's dark. Looking at my watch, I see it's late morning. I shrug and go inside to make more coffee. Why not? As the coffee is perking, I make a decision. I will continue searching the area and talking to people and discover who knows what about my childhood. *What in the world happened all those years ago?* If I'm going to stick around, it's important that I know what happened. Seems the ghosts of the past are haunting this house, the barns, and the sooner I put the pieces of the puzzle together, the faster the ghosts will disappear.

When the coffee is ready, I pour a mug and walk into the playroom, setting my mug on a nearby shelf. I stand there for a minute, wondering where I should start. There are so many boxes, so I dive in. Forgetting my coffee, I rifle through boxes of old games and puzzles, used coloring books, containers of crayons, old notebooks . . .

Wait. Notebooks! I pull a red notebook from the pile and sit on the floor with it. Inside are several pages of drawings—done by a child, it seems—mostly of castles and princes and princesses, some with dragons. These must be *my* old drawings. I look around the room, feeling a little defeated and lost. I'm not sure what I was hoping to find in those notebooks. Or in this room. But at least I explored a little. Now I know I can throw all this stuff away. I'm again wondering why on earth my parents kept all of this.

I stand and walk over to a shelf with more games and toys—Smurf figurines, a few My Little Pony dolls, an Etch A Sketch, things I vaguely remember. I leave those and reach for a box from the shelf, and a few books fall to my feet. I pick one up and smile. *Nancy Drew.* I used to read my mother's old books about the sly female detective. I can't believe I remember that! I must have been an advanced reader at eight years old. I set the book down and peer on the shelf where I had just pulled the box when I see some loose papers. As I look at them, I gasp. There are drawings of a little girl and a little boy. Holding hands, swimming, climbing a tree. Who is the little boy? Jeff? It seems he may be the key to the secrets of my past.

CHAPTER 9

"DARN!"

I yank the pot off the burner and throw it in the sink, burning my hand in the process. I burned the vegetables. Who burns vegetables? I've never quite learned how to cook properly, but goodness, it's frozen vegetables! Oh, how my mother would shake her head and scoff at me. "A woman's place," she had told me more than once, "is in the house—to bear children, to keep up the housework, and above all, cook and bake for her family." Growing up, I had realized how old-fashioned my mother sounded when she said that. I knew the basics of the kitchen—we all took turns at the home—but I never felt it was "my place" to be a proper cook unless I chose to be. And I had not chosen to be, thank you very much!

"Well, at least the chicken—"

An alarm sounds before I can open the oven door, and I run to the smoke detector hanging on the wall by the living room door, then wave a dish towel at it. Once the alarm is silenced, I smell something burning, and it's not vegetables.

"*No!*" I scream in frustration and run back to the oven. Taking the oven mitts, I pull the door open and choke on black smoke that is pouring out. The chicken is ruined.

After opening the door and window, I plop down on a chair and place my head in my hands. I ruined dinner. Thankfully, it's still the afternoon, so I can scrounge something up later. I'm just disappointed in myself. I had wanted to get my meal prep out of the way. Oh well. Good thing I'm not married. He'd certainly have to be the cook.

"Knock-knock!"

I jump at the sound of a man's voice. It's Sam, and he's standing in the doorway holding a casserole dish.

"Oh, Sam. Hi. Um . . ." I look nervously around the smoke-filled kitchen. Now I am mortified. I turn back to face him, but he only grins.

"Good thing you burned dinner. I brought a casserole over." He holds the dish out like it's a peace offering. I take it and smile, taking a whiff of the amazing smell coming from the dish. "It's Sheperd's pie. My grandma's recipe," he explains.

The dish almost falls out of my hands, but Sam grabs it and sets it on the counter, giving me a peculiar—if not annoyed—look. "Melissa, are you ok?"

I am *not* ok. Snickerdoodles, now Sheperd's pie. It's all so familiar—things I had as a child . . . but not just your typical "things you've eaten as a child" stuff. No, those things came from someone I knew in the past—someone close to me. Jeff, maybe? It has to be. Rachel said we were best friends. And he was my neighbor.

"Hey, look," Sam says, still standing in the doorway. He's dressed casually in jeans and a T-shirt but still seems so put together and sophisticated, just the way he holds himself. Far from what I am, I'm guessing. "I was wondering if you wanted to take a walk, get some fresh air. Maybe you can tell me about this area where you grew up."

I realize I'm staring, and I clear my throat. "Yes, that would be nice." I still feel dumbfounded by the food he keeps mentioning that brings me back to the past somehow but shake it off. Well, I might as well take a walk with a man who is practically a stranger to me. Why not.

I slip on my sneakers and follow Sam out the front door. The sun is, indeed, coming out from behind the clouds and the afternoon has warmed up. It's warm enough that jeans and my lightweight flannel shirt are perfect for being outdoors. Sam doesn't seem bothered wearing a T-shirt. New York weather is strange, so I never take chances. I realize I don't know where Sam came from, where he grew up. Maybe from New York like I did. Who knows.

"Well, where do you suggest we walk?" Sam asks, looking around.

I think about the road, but even though we're in the country, cars and trucks go about a hundred miles an hour here, and it seems busier than when I was a child—from what I remember, anyway. I turn and face the barns. They're standing tall, no shadows or darkness around them. What had I expected?

"Let's walk down there," I suggest while pointing to the path that leads around the barns to the property in the back. Maybe that will trigger some more memories for me.

"So, this looks like a path for a tractor or machinery," Sam comments as we head down the driveway and veer to the right side of the barn on the end. The cornfield is to our right, and after we pass the barns, there are cornfields on both sides of us. The path is no longer the driveway but a dirt road of sorts that must have been made by my father when he farmed.

"Yeah, I think so," I mutter, hoping to drum up some

memories.

As we walk, I see some tractors that are rusty and probably broken down. Not much further, we come to a place where the path splits—a cornfield on the left and trees to the right. In front of us is a steep hill, trees surrounding the path, and I see a small body of water at the bottom.

"Come on! Let's wade and look for minnows!!" I called out to my best friend and ran down the hill with my bucket, laughing playfully.

The creek stood before us, and we turned to each other and grinned before running through it. The sun warmed us as we splashed around in our bare feet before realizing we were scaring the minnows away.

My eyes widen, and I turn to look at Sam. "The creek. That's the creek I used to play in. Come on!"

And then, just like a kid, I begin to laugh and run down the hill. I hear Sam's footsteps behind me and feel my heart hammering in my chest. These visions, memories, I keep having are of me and another child. It must be Jeff! I'm feeling happy that things are coming back to me. For years, my therapists told me the past doesn't matter, I should move on, but why wouldn't I want to know why I left my home when I was so young? Who wouldn't want to know what happened? Closure. I just need closure.

I reach the bottom of the hill, and Sam stops next to

me, panting. The creek is basically a mini-sized pond with all sizes of stones throughout it, with its water spreading out on both sides like little rivers. The creek is too big to jump over when it's full but shallow enough to wade through, the water coming to our ankles. To our right sits a large boulder at the edge of a path next to the creek, and a rickety wooden bridge is close by. I walk to the boulder and sit. I remember a little now. I was here. I came here often with a little boy. Jeff. It had to be.

I close my eyes, feeling the sun's warmth against my face and the breeze whisking me to another place. Barefooted children, catching minnows, laughing gaily, and getting soaked as they splashed around. I smile at the thought.

"It's beautiful." Sam whispers the words as if not wanting to jolt me out of wherever I was just then.

I open my eyes and glance over at him. He is staring at the creek but isn't smiling, and his eyes are downcast. Sam sure is a mystery. I realize I don't know a thing about him. Good-looking. Serious. Mysterious for sure. But there's something else. Something I can't put my finger on. Or maybe I'm just conjuring up things that aren't there. He's a nice guy and seems harmless.

"So, Sam," I start, trying to learn a little more about him.

"Where are you from?"

He doesn't move for a second, and I wonder if he's in the same trance I seemed to be in when thinking about good times down here. Then he looks over at me.

"Oh! What's that?"

I turn my head to see what he's pointing at, then look back at him, knowing he is trying to distract me from asking about him. Fine. I'll play along.

I stand up, stretch, and walk over to the bridge, carefully placing my foot on the first board to test it. Only about six or eight boards are going across, so I skip over them. On the other side is a slight hill that leads up to cornfields, the path veering to the left. I turn to make sure Sam is following.

We walk up the slope and follow the trail, trees lining the left side of the path and a cornfield on the other side. We walk silently, except for the birds chirping, and come to a grove of trees with a patch of grass in the center. The day is warming up, and I'm sweating a little. I'm not bothered, though. I know the New York winter will be here soon enough.

"Looks like someone tried to build a tree fort here," Sam comments, pointing to one of the trees.

A wooden ladder—too short to reach the branches—leans against one tree, and as we inspect further, I see some tools and rusty buckets. Near another tree, almost hiding behind it, is a dolly with some different size boards lying across it. Someone was trying to build something here. A tree fort? Was it me and the little boy?

Suddenly, the kid in me feels playful, so I climb the five steps of the ladder, my arms reaching out to the lowest branch, and I latch on, pulling my body up. My feet reach the branch, and I pull myself up farther and then to the next few branches, finally sitting on the sturdiest one I see.

"Melissa, be careful up there!"

I look down at Sam and see a worried look on his face. I close my eyes, ignoring his warning. The warm sun on my body and the feeling of freedom up in this tree takes me back . . .

"Hey, no fair. I can't reach!"

I looked down at my best friend and frowned. Darn. He's right. He's too short even on the last rung of the ladder.

"Ok," I called down. "I'll have to find another ladder in Daddy's barn."

"Come down now, Melissa. We're only kids. You'll get hurt!"

"Spoil sport!" I yelled back. "We're going to build a fort here, so you better put your brave pants on!" He was being such a baby.

I was swinging my legs back and forth, when suddenly, as I went to lean back, my hands missed the branch and I felt myself falling.

"Melissa!"

I'm suddenly in Sam's arms. My eyes widen and fill with tears as he gently sets me on the ground. The sudden stumble and the waves of memories trying to make their way back to me are overwhelming. My feelings are crashing over me, causing hot tears to flood my eyes—stinging the insides of my nose with their saltiness. *Jeff. He had been my best friend. But who* was *he?*

"Are you ok?" Sam whispers, looking at me closely.

Our faces are so close I can almost feel his breath. We look into each other's eyes for a moment too long, and I break the moment by backing up and taking a deep breath to calm myself down. His eyes are so familiar. I can't shake that feeling.

I push the hair from my eyes, wishing I had thought to pull it up in a ponytail and look at him sheepishly.

"I . . . yeah. Wow. Sorry about that."

"You could have gotten hurt. Let's go back. It's getting chilly anyway."

It's not chilly at all, but I ignore the comment and follow Sam back down the path toward the creek, over the bridge, then up the hill back to my house. I feel like a chastened child. I certainly am not too old or out of shape to climb a tree. I almost fell because I was lost in a memory, that's all.

I then remembered what my therapist had warned me. *"Melissa, be careful out there. You're going to get triggers; memories will start coming through, and you may find yourself lost in them for a moment or a few minutes. Stay safe; don't put yourself anywhere that danger can lurk."*

We reach the house, and I look at Sam, feeling embarrassed. "Sorry, Sam. I guess a memory was triggered, and I lost track of where I was," I say sheepishly.

"What did . . . What did you remember?" he asks, his eyes narrowing slightly.

His demeanor startles me a bit, but I shrug it off. "I, uh, well just something about a tree fort, that's all." I am not going to tell a stranger what I remembered.

"Well, I guess I'll head home. I've got some work to do."

Oh. That was abrupt. I shift on my feet, wondering if I should say what I think I'm going to say and then just do it.

"Do you want to stay for dinner? I hear there's a delicious Sheperd's pie inside." I try to smile, but it seems forced. Maybe Sam can sense it because he smiles and shakes his head.

"Another time. You enjoy." He waves and heads back toward his house. I watch him for a moment, then hurry inside and close the door.

CHAPTER 10

"***MELISSSSSAAAAAA.***"

I jump up, not realizing I am on the couch, and nearly fall to the floor. Someone was whispering my name. But there's no one here! The house is dark, and it is quiet. *Too quiet.* I stand and reach for the lamp next to the couch and light fills the room. Had I fallen asleep, or did I get pulled into one of my memories again? I remember lying down to rest. Goodness, I must have been tired.

But who whispered my name? Maybe it was a dream. Yes, that must be it. It seemed so real, though. So close.

Convinced that it was all in my head, I stretch and walk into the kitchen, pulling the light on and looking around. Strange, I don't remember leaving the casserole dish with the Sheperd's pie on the table. Only . . . it isn't just sitting on the table alone. The dish is at the head of the table, where my father once sat, a clean plate and utensils next to it. *What the hell?*

I open the door and peek outside, but it's dark. I stand on the porch, looking through the screen door. Everything is dark except for a small light across the road, meaning Sam is home. *Of course he is home, silly*, I chide myself. *Where would he be? Here?*

I shake my head and walk back inside. "Better heat a plate of this up and eat something," I tell myself. I take a spoon and pull some of the casserole out and plop it onto the dish. Before I can warm it up, I notice steam coming from the food as well as the dish. *What?* I put my finger in the food and yank it back. It's hot!

I take two steps to the counter and grab a knife from the butcher block. Someone must be in the house. *Who warmed this up? Who called my name?*

I hear a thump. It sounded like it was outside. No way am I going out there in the dark . . . in the country. Wild animals or—worse—murderers could be out there! I wonder if there are wolves up in this area and I shiver a little. I'd hate to encounter a hungry wolf. Then again, would a murderer be any better? Ugh.

I turn back to the table and decide not to eat the

Sheperd's pie in case someone *did* sneak in and poison it. Irrational, maybe, but I will not take any chances here.

I dump the food into the trash and put the dishes in the sink. My eye catches something from the window that looks out at the cornfields. Is that a light? I squint, trying to see better, but the kitchen light is reflecting off the window. That must be it. The kitchen light. Reflecting.

I briefly think about calling 911, but the last time I did that, the two cops who came here seemed to think I was crazy—or drunk—so I'm not about to do that again. Not unless I really have to. So, because I am no longer hungry but need to calm my nerves, I hurry to the refrigerator and grab a bottle of wine. Probably not the best idea; I should keep my head, after all. But I pour a generous glass anyway, then light a candle and turn the kitchen light off. The candle sits on the counter, so it won't reflect off the window. I stand to the side of the sink slightly so no one outside can see me.

This is ridiculous, I think, taking a sip of my wine, letting the cool liquid run down my throat. I feel my nerves settling a little bit and I relax. I don't see any lights in the cornfield, which means I was imagining it.

I sit, drinking my wine and recounting the events of the day. Memory triggers, Sam's strange behavior, the Sheperd's pie. What is going on in this house?

The kitchen isn't feeling safe anymore, so I walk into the living room and sit down with my glass, then close my eyes and sip on my wine, leaning my head back, listening to the creaks and groans of the house. My nerves are shot, I think. I don't know if I can stay here alone.

"*Melisssssaaaaaa.*"

I hear the voice again and jump, dropping my wine glass. "Damnit!" I yell to the empty house. "If you're trying to scare me, it's not working!" It actually *is* working, but damn if I'm going to admit that! I pick up my glass, ticked that the wine is now soaking through the old, musty carpet, and when I stand up, I see someone standing on the other side of the living room window.

Then I scream.

CHAPTER 11

"MELISSA? HEY, MELISSA."

I moan and turn my head. *Where am I?* As my eyes open, I see Sam kneeling over me. *Sam? What's he doing here? What happened?*

"No, no," Sam says softly as I try to sit up. "Just relax."

I lie there for a minute, then sit up, Sam's hand on my back. I look around. I'm in the living room, near the couch. Both lamps are lit and the curtains are closed. *How did the curtains get closed? Did I close them? Did Sam close them? I swear they were open. Weren't they?* My head hurts.

"What the hell happened?" I turn to Sam in confusion.

"I was checking the mail because I forgot earlier, and I heard you scream," Sam explains. "When I got here, you were crouched down beside the couch, hysterical."

Oh. Well, that's embarrassing. I stand and brush my jeans off, looking into Sam's eyes. I wish I had good discernment. I wish I could read people. Sam is definitely a mystery to me. And how could he have heard me from his mailbox? I know it's on the same side of the road as my house, but I can't imagine he'd hear me from there. Had my scream been that loud?

He's staring at me, so I guess I should say something.

"Thanks for checking on me. You didn't . . . You didn't happen to come over earlier, did you?"

Sam frowns. "Yes, I was here earlier. I brought you the Sheperd's pie, remember?"

"Yes, I know that, but did you come over when . . . Well, when I was sleeping on the couch? It's just that when I went to the kitchen, someone had set a place at the table, and the pie was hot, like someone heated it." Sam just stares at me. "I mean," I hurry to continue so I don't offend him, "if you did, that's fine, I just . . ." I laugh a little. Maybe I *am* going crazy.

"Are you sure you're ok by yourself here?" Sam asks.

I walk into the kitchen and stop short. After tossing the Sheperd's pie, I put the dishes in the sink. Now, the casserole dish is sitting on the table, empty.

What. The. Hell. Is. Going. On?

"Melissa?"

I spin around and point my finger at Sam, forgetting that a moment ago he had such a sympathetic look in his eyes.

"You. You did this. You're trying to make me crazy so I'll be sent away."

"What? Lissy, I don't know what you're—"

"*Lissy?* No one calls me that!"

No one has since—

"I'm sorry." Sam puts his hands up in surrender. "Look, Melissa, you're just on edge, that's all. Sometimes living alone—especially in a really old and creepy house as this one—can cause . . . well, things to go on in your mind that aren't really true."

I take a few deep breaths, trying to calm down, but it's not working. My entire body is shaking with nerves. Something isn't right here. Maybe his kind eyes and nice gestures are to sway me—to get me to believe he's someone else, not someone dangerous. I back up a little, now feeling more nervous than before.

"Look, I don't know what happened, or what you think happened, but I'm trying to be nice here."

I almost detect a hint of defense in his words. I start to soften a bit, thinking I'm just overreacting. Again. This house is getting to me, that's all. Too many secrets; too much trying to remember.

I take a breath. "I'm sorry. I just got spooked again. It's this house."

"Look, I know you don't know me, but why don't you come over and we'll have some tea, see if we can calm those nerves of yours?"

My eyes widen slightly. Sam is practically a stranger! I think for a moment, and I realize I *would* like to see inside the house he lives in. It's been there since my childhood, though I don't remember being inside.

"Ok . . ." I say slowly, against any better judgment that I may have. "Let me grab a sweater."

A minute later, I'm heading across the road in the dark, with a man I just recently met. I must be crazy. Or maybe I just want to get out of that damn house.

I study the house before me as Sam and I walk up the steep driveway. My head hurts as my mind tries to conjure up memories. I stare, hoping to trigger a memory from childhood, but nothing comes. Everything is quiet around us; not even the sound of a cricket or an owl can be heard. The leaves from the maple trees rustle in the slight breeze. The vast lawns on either side of the house are dark, and I quicken my steps to catch up with Sam.

"This way." Sam walks ahead through the garage, where

there's a door leading into the house. Two other doors sit on other walls for exits to the outside.

I walk up the three steps and into the house, closing the door behind me. I'm standing in a small entrance with a door to my left, and in front of me is the kitchen, all open concept. I can see the dining room and living room straight ahead. I step into the kitchen, and to my left along the wall is another door—a bedroom?—and I assume a hallway leading to the bathroom and other bedrooms. It's a cute house. Perfect for a single man or someone wanting to start a family. I wonder briefly about the family who lived here before.

Sam wastes no time setting the kettle on the stove and preparing the tea. Once it's steeped, he hands a cup to me and heads to the living room. I follow, glancing around. The house is very . . . sparse. Simple furniture but nothing on the walls—no clock or pictures.

Sam sits on the leather recliner, which is against one wall, and I sit on the leather couch. The living room has a coffee table, the couch and recliner, and a television, but that's it. No plants. No carpet—the house seems to be all wood flooring. It's cold, this open area. And I don't mean temperature.

Sam sips on his tea and I follow suit, not wanting to

seem too eager for memories. I lean back on the couch, relaxing a bit.

"So, Melissa," Sam says. "Tell me about the house you grew up in. It seems very old. Could it be, pray tell, haunted?" He wiggles his eyebrows, suggesting he's joking, but his eyes look serious.

"Who knows? I left when I was a child. I remember certain things, but not all. Mostly I don't remember people or . . ." I pause. Dare I say, "Or what happened all those years ago" and leave myself open for more questions? After all, I don't know this man from Adam, though he seems nice. I almost laugh at my last thought. *Of course he seems nice; kidnappers and serial killers are nice from the start. I don't think.*

"So, you don't remember anything that happened? I mean, why would you abruptly leave as a child?"

I sit up. "I didn't say I left abruptly."

Sam chuckles, draining the rest of his tea. *Is he blushing?* "Oh, yes, I know that. It just seems . . ." He doesn't finish, simply picks up my mug, which is still half full, and goes into the kitchen to add more. This doesn't thrill me; I'm really not fond of tea.

It's then that I notice there's a sliding glass door between the couch and the chair, a curtain covering the inside so I can't see in. I wonder what that room is. I stand to walk over, but Sam appears and shoves the mug into my hand, gesturing to the couch. I dutifully sit, feeling slightly embarrassed that I was about to try to peek into a stranger's room without permission.

"Sorry," I mumble. "That's a curious door. Sliding glass doors inside?" I subconsciously twirl a bit of my hair with my finger, glancing at the door.

"Maybe it's an addition that was built on." Sam shrugs and sits down.

"You haven't been—"

"So, your house . . ." He interrupts me, clearly evading the pending question.

How has he not been in that room since he moved in here? Something is strange. But I let it go. For now. Instead, I say, "My house is old, yes. Haunted? I don't think so." I laugh a little and drink my tea, grimacing at the taste. I cannot wait to finish this disgusting concoction and leave.

Sam chuckles and we start chatting like we're old friends, and I find myself relaxing a bit. I tell him a little of what I do remember of my childhood—my father a farmer, my mother a housewife, a grandma, no brothers or sisters—and he tells me he's an only child and is a writer of paranormal. I am intrigued. No wonder he asked if my house was haunted. I try to get him to talk more about his writing career—is he published?—but he evades the questions and asks more about my house. I wonder if I don't find that terribly peculiar now because he claims to be a writer of paranormal. Still, it's a bit unsettling that he only seems to want to talk about my house . . . "How many bedrooms," and "What's the attic like?" Things like that. I don't give him too much information; I simply tell him I am not sure because I haven't really gone through all the rooms yet. Gee, he's nosey!

After we finish our tea, Sam excuses himself to use the restroom. When he is out of sight, I quickly stand and step in front of the mysterious sliding glass door. It had been on my mind during our chat, and I'm dying to see what's inside! I check the handle and am thrilled to find it unlocked. Taking a glance to my left to make sure Sam hasn't reappeared, I lift the latch and carefully slide the door open just a few inches, the slight creaking sound making me pause to make sure Sam hasn't heard.

When satisfied that he's still out of earshot, I lift the latch the rest of the way up and pull the door open. It slides easily, and before I know it, I'm looking into a small room that is stuffy and warm, and it has a very musty smell. Straight ahead is a door—the kind you'd see on someone's porch—and to the right are two big windows. To the left is a small window with curtains behind it. There must be a room on the other side of that wall because that leads to the house. How strange. The carpet is red and looks quite worn. The room—though it is obviously some sort of addition and seems strange with the sliding glass doors—is pretty normal, except . . .

The entire room is full of boxes and toys. Old toys from the looks of it. There's a plastic castle of some sort with figurines scattered around it, a few things that look like games, a near deflated ball, stuffed animals, toy cars . . .

I hear footsteps and quietly slide the door back and push the latch down, then hurry over to the kitchen just as Sam appears.

"Not leaving yet, are you?"

"Oh, it's getting late, and I should try to get some rest."

"Can I walk you home?"

I laugh at that. "I think I'll be ok. Anyway, thank you for the tea."

"Anytime, Melissa." Sam grins and opens the door for me.

I give a wave and then head down the driveway, thinking Sam might not be so bad after all. Sure, he's odd, but he could say the same about me. What is *normal,* anyway?

The night air is cool and only a half-moon and some stars light the sky. As I reach the end of the driveway, I glance back to Sam's house. He's standing in the window but notices that I'm looking. He doesn't wave, simply stares. *Does he know I opened the door to the—is it a playroom?* The toys looked old. I mean, they looked well-used and not quite of this day and age. Then again, I haven't been to a toy store at all, so what would I know? *But why would he keep them in the house that he bought?* I shake my head. I am too imaginative for my own good. He probably hasn't had a chance to get a dumpster and get rid of them yet. Maybe he doesn't care since he doesn't seem intent on staying for long.

As I hurry across the empty street, the distant howling grows louder. My eyes dart nervously toward the looming house ahead, its windows dark and haunting. Goosebumps rise on my skin as the wind picks up, carrying a chill through the air. To be honest, I don't relish entering this house alone right now. Shadows dance around the trees, like ghosts playing a prank. Waiting. Watching.

I hurry into the house and slam the door behind me.

CHAPTER 12

"***RELAX AND TAKE*** *your time, Melissa. This is a safe place for children."*

I laid on the small couch, my feet barely reaching the end, and closed my eyes while Dr. Hanson spoke. I did feel safe there, and I liked my doctor. He was nice. He had been my doctor for the six months I'd been there. "The safe house," Mommy calls it, though it is bigger than a normal house. It has a big sitting room, a kitchen, a huge library, some bedrooms and other normal house things, but it's so big!

I took some deep breaths and waited for Dr. Hanson to talk.

"Ok, now I want you to tell me some fun things you remember from your house on the farm."

Deep breaths. Breathe in. Exhale slowly. Dr. Hanson waited.

Finally, I said, "I played a game. Ring Around the Rosie. It was fun."

"That is a popular game," Dr. Hanson said.

"I loved running down to the creek and having picnics and catching minnows." I giggled a little at the memory.

Dr. Hanson smiled. "The barns, Melissa. You played in the barns, right?"

"Yes," I whispered.

I didn't want to do this anymore. I wanted to be in my room, where it was safe. Breathe in. Exhale. Breathe in. Exhale.

"Melissa," Dr. Hanson said softly but firmly. "You loved the barns. What about . . . the silo?"

I sat up and looked Dr. Hanson straight in the eyes, my eyes narrowing as I said, "We do not talk about the silo."

* * * * *

I wake up, my pajamas sticking to my body from sweat. I push the covers off and sit up, itching to shower and get into some clean clothes. The clock tells me it's already six in the morning, so I climb out of bed and breathe deeply, trying to slow my racing heart. Perhaps I should have accepted the antianxiety pills offered to me before I returned. No. I need my wits about me. I need to stay focused.

The dream is unnerving, remembering that session with Dr. Hanson. He wanted to talk about something I didn't even remember. He insisted my subconscious was holding back; repression, he called it. I think I simply don't remember. The silo. The barns. Why did he bring those up? The thought of them scared me at the time. Even my parents didn't let me talk about the silo after they moved me to a special place after my coma. So why would Dr. Hanson want to talk about it?

When it seemed like I wasn't recalling much, my therapist suggested I begin moving forward instead of trying to look back. How could I do that, though, when I could barely remember anything? I still can't! Not much, anyway. Not only that, but I want to know why I was sent away to live without my parents. Why my parents moved. *What happened that year that our lives were turned upside down? Why can't I remember much?*

Those are the answers I want—*the answers I need.* I deserve to remember. After all, I may be living here for a long time, so I'd rather face the past now.

The sun is out, but the thermometer reads sixty degrees, a little chilly for my liking. After a quick shower, and dressing in jeans and a T-shirt that has seen better days, I eat a light breakfast, forgoing the coffee since I'm too wound up already, and sit at the table, wondering what to do next. I've looked through the house, but I haven't really dug through boxes, and I haven't touched the attic. I wonder what is in there. That might be a good project for today. I'd love to find some photo albums or toys from the past. But first, I want to take a walk.

I head down the driveway and past the barns, walking toward the creek where Sam and I went. When I get to the bottom of the hill, I spot the large boulder that used to be my favorite place to sit, and I climb on it. I close my eyes, and suddenly, a sharp pain slices through my head.

"Why is it important to remember the past, Melissa?" Dr. Hanson asked almost impatiently. I'd been counseling with him for years now, and he insisted I stop trying to remember what happened. Funny, because when we started, he was trying to get me to remember!

I didn't say anything at first, just looked past him at the hideous painting on the wall. It looked like something a child would paint. I'm sure it cost a bundle too.

"Melissa?"

I looked at my therapist then. I'd love to remind him that when I first started seeing him, he was trying to get me to talk about the past—about things that frightened me—and I just couldn't speak of them but wasn't sure why. And now he is asking why I want to remember. Therapists don't make sense sometimes.

"At eight years old, I was removed from my home. I was in a coma. Now I'm here, having all sorts of therapies and not allowed to

go home. Why in the world wouldn't I want to remember?"

"The point here, Melissa, is to move on so that you can go back home. Eventually. When you're better."

I stood up quickly and started to pace the room. Such a dark room. But for a small lamp on my therapist's desk, there was no other light. He sat in his upright chair, and I was usually on the couch. But not now. I needed to pace. I needed to get the restlessness out.

"And who decides when I'm better? I've been here for years. I know how to live on my own. I know what I went through, and I am healed physically and emotionally. I just want to remember before I go back. I want to know what happened—how I was hurt and why I need all of this therapy!"

Dr. Hanson was silent for a second before he spoke. "Sometimes healing comes from moving on. I do believe you're almost ready to go home, to leave this place. But the memories you could potentially gain could be dangerous. I feel it's best to move forward and not look at the past."

I shook my head in disagreement. So many things had been kept from me. I felt I couldn't move forward until I knew what had happened in the past. But even if no one told me, or I didn't remember, I'd find out eventually. I'd go back home and find out.

I sigh and open my eyes, glancing around me. The green leaves and grass are starting to change in anticipation of fall, and birds flit about. It's so peaceful down here. I don't want to leave, but I know I must head back to the house and start looking around, maybe sorting through things to start cleaning up and ridding of useless junk. Because the truth is, I might leave some day. It's just too strange being back here.

When I get back to the house, I grab a flashlight so I can explore. I noticed, the other day while walking around the house, the attic window was broken, so who knows what animal—or animals—got in.

I walk down the hall to the attic door and turn the knob. It gives a loud creek and I yank the door open.

"Oh. My. Gosh."

I stand in the doorway, almost not believing the sight before me. The attic is packed. No—it's *jam packed.* I step inside but can barely get one foot in. I can't even see the floor! I shake my head and glance around. Piles of stuff from floor to ceiling are on both sides, and I can barely see a "path" to the back, where there's a window. I can't even explain what "stuff" is around; it seems mostly garbage bags, boxes, and furniture, though I catch some glimpses of toys and strange items I can't identify.

I start to walk through, kicking bags, boxes, and toys out of my way. The air is warm and thick, and the smell . . . Well, I can only describe it as *old.* Sort of musty, but . . .

something I can't put my finger on. *I really hope there aren't any dead animals in here.* My stomach churns.

I finally reach the end. I notice a door on each of the two walls. Curious. First, I look at the window. The glass is shattered, so I'll have to get that fixed soon. Don't want birds or squirrels to get in. Or bats. Unless they already are. I shudder at the thought.

I turn to the door on my left. It's a small door—the height of a child, really—and when I open it, I can barely see inside. There are a few boxes, but that's all I can make out. I back out of that and close the door then go to the opposite side of the room to the other small door. This one also holds boxes, but I notice something on the floor.

My hand grazes over a cold copper handle, and then I realize . . . It's a trap door! I pull up on the handle with a grunt, forcing it open. The trap door creaks open and reveals a dark hole below. As I peer into the darkness, my hand fumbles around my pocket for my flashlight. My heart races as I click the switch, but the light doesn't come on. Panic sets in as I continue to click frantically, but nothing happens. In a last-ditch effort, I shake the flashlight and slap it against my hand. The light flickers on. A wave of relief washes over me as I am no longer in complete darkness.

The thin beam of light illuminates a set of narrow steps

leading down into the unknown. The pungent odor of staleness immediately assaults my senses as I cautiously make my way through the stifling darkness and down the steps, each one groaning beneath my weight. The air is thick and musty, clinging to every surface and making it difficult to breathe. It is as if time has stood still in this forgotten place, covered in a layer of decay that seems almost . . . overwhelming. But I press on, determined to uncover whatever secrets lay hidden within these walls, swiping at imaginary (or not) cobwebs.

When I reach the bottom, there's a door. It sticks a little, but when I push it open, I find myself staring at the "old part of the house," which is what used to be the original house before the addition. I never knew there were stairs that led to the attic. Then again, I was a child last time I was home, so why would I know? I hadn't needed to.

I step into the room and close the door behind me. When I turn around, I'm facing the stairs that I just came from and see a door on either side. I peek into one room, the walls painted a hideous blue-green color, my eyes widening. It's filled with junk! I only see piles of furniture and trash bags. The same with the room on the other side of the stairs. I turn back around and shake my head. But for a tool bench lining one side of the wall, it's all boxes and bags, outdoor furniture, more old toys . . . just junk. Junk,

junk, junk! I want to scream. Why did my parents leave me with all of this? Why had they stored it all? What the hell was the point?

"Get a grip, Melissa," I mutter to myself. I guess I have my work cut out for me, throwing all of this out. Maybe I can hire someone to help. Or not. It's too embarrassing. I'd rather do it alone. Though it seems like taking a match to the house would be easier.

I walk over to one door that I know leads outside and notice it's slightly ajar. "Odd," I mumble.

Then I look down. There are footprints from dirt on the floor. I follow the tracks, noticing they lead to the other door that must go into the house. They must be recent. Footprints would not last, right? I have no idea. All I know is they're in front of me, and I'm scared.

I cover my mouth to stifle a scream and look around wildly. *Is someone here? Have they been watching me? Or maybe they're outside?* Broken windows, doors off their hinges, rooms filled with *stuff*. It's a haven for anyone who wants shelter, or worse . . . *murder*.

Breathing deeply, I creep to the front of the room and carefully peer out the window. Nothing. No one. I reach in my back pocket for my cell phone and quickly dial 911. This is getting ridiculous. Someone is messing with me!

Within twenty minutes—I could have been murdered in the meantime!—a cop car pulls up. I step forward from where I was huddled on the old porch and notice it's the same damn officer—Monroe, aka Giganto—climbing out of the car. A woman who appears to be in her thirties, dark skinned, and absolutely beautiful, climbs out of the other side. She is small but looks like she could kick some ass if she needed to.

Officer Giganto steps toward me, but I am looking at the woman instead. I'll talk to her. Maybe *she* won't think I'm crazy.

"Thank you for coming," I say, keeping some respectable distance between us. I don't want her to think I'm a threat.

"I'm Officer Ellis."

I start to say "Nice to meet you," but she immediately goes into business mode. "So you saw footprints?" She's glancing at the house.

I don't feel threatened by her in the least, so I don't even look at Giganto. "Yep." Then I proceed to tell her things that I've seen and heard since I came back. She listens attentively and nods in all the right places. Out of the corner of my eye, I see the other officer looking around.

"We'll take a look," Giganto says. Then the two officers leave me standing there.

I'm not sure what to do, so I sit at the outdoor table and wait. The sunny, cloudless day is warming, and though my leg is shaking with nervousness and anticipation, I'm wanting the coffee I never made this morning.

As usual, it's quiet but for a few country sounds—birds, dogs in the distance, a few cars here and there—and of course all is quiet across the road. I'd half expected Sam to come over after seeing a patrol car in front of my house. He's probably home, after all, trying to work on his book. I know I'd be curious if I saw police at his house. Heck, he gets curious if he sees my light go off!

After what seems like an eternity, the officers are finally walking toward me with faces I can only describe as skeptical. *Great. They don't believe me.*

"Ms. Turner," Officer Giganto says, almost sounding bored. *Oh, I could slap him!* "We did see the footprints, but there's no sign of a break-in. We checked all entries to the house, including windows. Nothing."

"But—"

"Maybe a nearby farmer wanted to take a look at the land, a neighbor, perhaps—could have been anyone. But if someone really wanted to hurt you, they'd have done it."

So that's it. They didn't see a person and are fluffing off the footprints and all the other stuff I told them about.

Great. Just great.

"We'll have another officer monitor the area, drive by a few times throughout the rest of the day and tonight, but my guess is whoever got into the porch won't come back. Maybe they realized someone is living here and left. A squatter, perhaps."

That does not settle my nerves, but what can I do? Yet another police visit and nothing to show for it. Not that I want a serial killer or squatter or whoever, but it would explain things. At least they saw the footprints. Can't say I'm terribly crazy now.

I'm about to nod and thank them when Giganto speaks up. "Ms. Turner," he says in a slightly condescending tone.

"Melissa," I snap.

He clears his throat and continues. "I did a little searching. Seems you've come from a slightly troubled past. You were in a facility after being in a coma. Is that correct?"

My cheeks burn, and I ball my hands into fists. "I was, but that was because of an accident. I'm fine now. They released me. I'm fine to be on my own," I practically hiss. I'm wondering why any of this even matters! I called them to find an intruder, not interrogate me, my past.

He only nods, which is maddening. "Look," he says slowly, looking me in the eyes. There's not an ounce of compassion in his. He clears his throat, then says, "You probably are fine to be on your own. But given your past, and the fact that you live out here alone . . . well, it's natural that you may see things. Hear things."

Officer Ellis at least has the decency to look away, slightly embarrassed. How *dare* Giganto? He is basically accusing me of being a nutty woman living on her own and seeing things. Hearing things. Shame on him. Shame on the system! I've had it with the system.

We stand there for what seems like a full minute when I realize they're not going to do or say anything else. So I mumble, "Thanks for checking," and then storm into the house and slam the door.

CHAPTER 13

I'M SO ANGRY after they leave, but I don't want to stew in anger or start drinking. Drinking was my outlet after I turned twenty-one and had my first taste of wine while out to dinner with a few of the other residents. Whenever I was feeling especially sad or confused because I missed my parents and had no idea what my childhood was like until I started regaining my memory, I would have some wine. Sometimes whiskey. But most of the time, it was wine. My doctors and therapists told me that was unhealthy, of course, and I knew in my heart it was. But it was my comfort. There are worse things. And do I really care about my liver? Goodness, I have no family here, no friends, and I'm seemingly going crazy. I should just drink myself to death.

I sigh, pushing that awful thought out of my head. Surely there's going to be more to my life someday. I'm sure I have a purpose. Well, for now, I feel I have to keep my wits about me out here in the country—in this creepy farmhouse, with the creepy barns. Coffee is out of the question, since I'm wound too tightly.

The barns, I think again. There's something about the barns that call to me, though. Sure, they're a bit eerie, and I know I've been spooked before by them, but I want to do a thorough search. Maybe I'll get a memory trigger. At the very least, I'll be able to see if there's any equipment left there. Maybe I can sell it to a local farmer.

I walk slowly down the path toward the barns, looking out at the cornfields and marveling at how the sun reflects off the corn stalks. I find it very pretty. Someday, I would like to be an artist so I can paint beautiful scenery. I wasn't gifted in that area, unfortunately.

A squirrel darts in front of me and runs into the shrubbery on one side of the barns, and I giggle a little. I suddenly remember chasing squirrels when I was young. Daddy would scold me, but my mom let me do it. She said squirrels were "dirty nuisances" and didn't want them near the house. And, of course, I thought chipmunks were the most adorable creatures! They never let me get close, though.

I head down to the lower portion of the main barn. It's long with several windows. The door is broken, half off its hinges, and hangs like a dangling fingernail. I step onto the concrete floor and stand there, taking in my surroundings. I'm in a short hallway, and to my right is a small room that I remember vividly, but I can't recall who I used to play with here. Perhaps it was the little boy in the picture I drew, or maybe it was the neighbor that Rachel mentioned—Jeff. I think it's a good idea to reach out to Rachel's sister, Megan, to see if she can help jog my memory. I've been having more and more flashbacks, but I'd love to know more about Jeff other than the fact that we played together.

I step into the small room and look up with a smile. Yep, it's still there—the square hole in the ceiling at the far wall. The ledge from the window allowed us to step up, then grab the ceiling beam and hoist ourselves onto the beams, which I used to walk across to get to the opening of the bigger barn. Amazing what the mind chooses to remember.

"Come on, slowpoke!"

"Well, I'm shorter than you," he huffed. "Gimme a break."

"Ok, catch me if you can!"

"Wait, Melissa! Wait for me. I don't want Bigfoot to catch me."

I laughed at that. We've never even seen Bigfoot. But Jeff was such a scaredy-cat. I thought boys were supposed to be brave! Jeff gave me a dirty look when I laughed.

Bigfoot? What in the world is a bigfoot?

I shake my head at the memory that ran through my head while staring at the hole. My head starts to ache, as it does sometimes with these memories. I take a few deep breaths and turn around to head back to the hallway.

I walk down to the bigger part of that barn, and I grin. This was where my dad kept all the cows! All the stalls are still here and even some old hay. I walk past each one, touching the cold steel posts and fondly thinking back on those cows, even the big plops of poop. I giggle a little at the thought. When I reach one end of the barn, I peer through the double doors into a wooded area that has some old machines and a large concrete structure that probably is a well or watering trough. I carefully step over large branches and dodge rusty metal pieces and soon find myself standing in a clearing, right next to one of the silos. I peer up at the large structure, and a cold chill courses through my body. Something flies into the small opening near the top and I squint. Is it a bird?

Suddenly, I hear a screeching sound and whip my head around. Nothing is there but the cornfield and the hill leading up to my house. Probably some animal or bird. I better get back to the house before it gets dark.

Back at the house, I slip my sneakers off when I hear a knock on the door.

"Melissa, it's me, Sam."

I open the door. Sam stands on the other side holding a tray of cookies, and he grins.

"Snickerdoodles!" He holds the tray out to me.

"Wow, oh . . . these look good." I step aside and gesture for him to come in.

Sam walks inside and sits at the table as if I had invited him to do so or like he was an old friend. Well, we had spent an evening chatting at his house. I guess I would consider him my friend.

I set the tray down and pour us some coffee. Once I sit, we each take a cookie. Its sugary goodness melts in my mouth, still warm and very soft. The cookie . . . It reminds me of something, yet my brain won't pull up the memory. *What* is it *about these cookies?*

"Good, eh?" Sam grins and grabs another one.

"Sure are. They taste familiar, like I've had them before."

Sam shrugs. "They're not entirely popular, but they beat the chocolate chip cookie, in my opinion."

"I agree."

"So, I saw you walking up from the barns a few minutes ago. Everything ok?" Sam takes a sip of his coffee, his eyes not meeting mine but darting around the kitchen like he's nervous. *He is a bit odd*, I think. Then again, maybe all writers are a bit odd. They'd have to be to be thinking of fiction all of the time—especially paranormal.

"Oh, just looking over the barns. I didn't get too far." I don't tell him it's because I got spooked.

"I'd be happy to go with you, if you'd like."

"Oh, sure. Yeah. That would be ok."

Sam grins. "I've never been in a barn before, especially one so old. It could be interesting."

I start to relax and grab another cookie. We talk about random things, and though I think maybe he is a bit odd, he's the only company I have right now.

"Well," Sam says, standing up after his second cup of coffee is finished. "I need to get back to work. Keep the cookies and enjoy."

"Thanks, Sam." I stand as well and open the door for him.

"See you around." Sam waves and walks out.

I watch as he darts across the lawn and the road, then runs up his driveway. He reaches the top and turns to wave before heading inside.

I close the door and stare at the tray of cookies. *Why are they so familiar to me?* I honestly cannot recall eating them in the last twenty-five years of my life. Though, to be fair to myself, I don't really have many memories. Hence the therapy.

* * * * *

Strange sounds keep me up at night. Creaking stairs, fluttering and scampering in the walls, like birds and mice, and outdoor sounds I'm not used to. Probably in my imagination. Stupid imagination. Maybe I *would* be a good writer. After all, I have the mind for it.

I can't sleep, so I climb out of bed and put my slippers on, intending on heading downstairs to make some tea, when suddenly, I hear footsteps. They're coming from the hallway, where the attic and my parents' old bedroom are.

Creak . . . creak . . .

Silence.

I'm frozen where I stand. *What do I do? The other stairway! I'll go down that way.*

I tiptoe hurriedly to the other door and carefully open it, praying it won't creak or squeak. Then I make haste through the darkness to the stairs that lead to the kitchen. I know those will make noise, so I take my slippers off and walk barefoot down each wooden step, my heart beating in my chest.

When I reach the bottom, I wait, listening. Nothing. I carefully peek through a gap in the slats, worrying that I'll see a pair of eyes staring back at me. I don't see that, thankfully. Just a kitchen void of ghosts and people.

Now what? Should I get a knife from the kitchen and wait? There's no way I can wait in the stairwell. The intruder could come up behind me and—well, hurt or kill me. I don't know their intention.

I take a breath and push the door open, the dark kitchen before me. I hate the dark. You never know what looms in darkness. I quickly turn on the kitchen light and then hurry into the living room, turning on both lamps. What I see in the corner jolts me, and my heart is pounding. Next to the woodstove is a stack of wood. *How did that get there?* There wasn't any wood next to the stove. I certainly didn't put it there!

I spin around, frantically looking for someone who may be hiding in that room. A sound draws me to the playroom, and I creep over, putting my hand on the doorknob. No. I can't go in. I don't have a weapon. Nothing to defend myself with. I back up and hurry into the kitchen. I grab the biggest butcher knife and sit at the kitchen table, my back to the refrigerator so the door to the staircase is on my left, the front door before me, and the living room to my right.

If there is someone here, I'll catch them.

* * * * *

My head is pounding. I'm so cold. *Where am I?*

I open my eyes and find that I'm in the living room, lying on the couch with only a light afghan covering my body. *How did I get here?* The last thing I remember is sitting at the kitchen table, knife in hand.

Where is the—

There. The knife is on the end table. Wow, I must be losing it. But what of the footsteps I heard? I slowly sit up and blink a few times. I'm blacking out. I must be. I remember coming downstairs early this morning in search of an intruder. I know I heard a sound like someone walking around. I sigh and push the afghan off my body and stand up. I need to get dressed, make coffee, and really get to the tasks on my list to figure out what happened long ago and then get the hell out of here! There's no way I can keep staying here with all this weird stuff going on. Someone must be messing with me. If they wanted to hurt me or steal something, they'd have done it by now.

I start walking to the kitchen when I glance over. What I see brings me to my knees.

There is no wood stacked by the woodstove.

CHAPTER 14

I AM SO shaken up by the strange occurrences of late that I barely sleep the next two nights, going from room to room in a zombie-like state, holding my butcher knife, looking for possible intruders. I cannot explain the stacked wood being next to the woodstove one minute and not there the next. Either someone is messing with me, or I'm losing my marbles. I briefly thought about calling the police again, but I fear that would make me look crazy, and I'm sure Giganto already thinks I am. So, I go it alone.

To keep myself busy during the days, I manage to clean out more junk from the laundry room and playroom. Most of it is just old clothing, shoes, tattered books, puzzles, and games with missing pieces. I'm wondering why my mother didn't get rid of it when she and Dad moved. Did she think I'd want it after all these years? I've no need for any of it, so I trash it. I rented a dumpster and am just tossing bags and bags into it.

It's now Saturday afternoon, and I just hauled two more bags out. I take a deep breath, loving the smell of the country air and taking in the bright sun. I'm certainly glad I moved back in the summer, even if it is almost fall.

"Looks like you've been busy."

I slightly jump and turn to Sam's voice. "Hey. I haven't seen you in a while. Been busy writing?"

He nods absently and peers into the dumpster. "Wow, there's a lot of stuff."

"Um, yeah." I chuckle a little. "So, what have you been up to other than writing?" I wipe my hands on my jeans and start walking toward the front door, hoping Sam follows. It's strange that he's so interested in my trash. Honestly, I am surprised at how much I've managed to toss. My mind went round and round, wondering why my parents kept the things they did.

"Just trying to get some work done. Sorry I've been a hermit."

"Yeah, I get it." I *don't* get it, but I'm not sure what else to say.

We stand there for a few awkward moments, neither of

us saying anything.

"It's a nice day," Sam finally says. "Why don't we take a walk? I'd love to see more of the land back there." He gestures to the barns.

"Oh, sure. Let me wash my hands and grab some water."

Ten minutes later, Sam and I are hiking down toward the creek again, only instead of walking down the hill to the water, we veer left and take the path along the tree line. It's so beautiful here. There are many bushes with berries starting to show, but I'm not sure what is poisonous and what isn't, so I leave them alone.

We walk in companionable silence when suddenly, Sam lightly taps my arm and says, "Race ya!" Then he takes off down the path.

I stand there in shock, trying to figure out what led to his childish behavior, but I quickly regain my composure and chase after him. We are both laughing while he occasionally looks back at me. I haven't run in . . . well, I don't know how long! But it feels good! I feel so carefree. The path leads to a hill, which we run up, and then we continue straight to the woods. Eventually, we reach a barbed-wire fence that lines the trees. I am pretty fast, and it seems like Sam is a bit out of shape. He is panting and laughing at the same time.

"Should we go in?" I gesture to the vast woods before us on the other side of the fence.

Sam's eyes widen for a second but then he grins. "Sure, why not?"

We find a spot where the fence wires are lower and jump over them. I doubt the wires are live anymore, but it would still hurt to get caught on one.

"Wow," I breathe, staring at an opening to the dark woods. The sun is out, but the trees are so dense it can barely sneak through to light the woods.

Sam starts walking into the opening and I quickly follow. I notice there's a path, slightly overgrown, and Sam heads down it as if he knows where it will lead. I look around while following. We are surrounded by tall trees, a lot of twigs and rocks, and unknown shrubs and leaves. I hear chattering of critters and the chirps of birds; otherwise, the forest is quiet.

Sam doesn't speak while he walks; he simply follows the path as if he has a purpose, and once in a while he looks around. I say nothing because I'm taking in my surroundings but also wondering what we'll find. *Who do these woods belong to? Do I own this land? Did it belong to my father? What are we doing here?*

"Um, Sam," I say, stuffing my hands in my pockets.

"Are we exploring or just walking the path to see where it leads us? I have no memory of these woods, and—"

"Shh!"

I startle when he cuts me off. His hand is out as if to stop me from walking. I do. Sam seems to be listening to something, so I strain my ears as well. I hear nothing.

"Look!" Sam whispers.

I turn my head to where he points and see nothing but dense forest. "What am I—"

"Shh!"

Oh, if this man "shooshes" me one more time!

I stand still and don't say a word. Suddenly, out of a nearby shrub, a creature bursts out and runs toward us! I start to run, not caring to see what the creature is, when something grabs my arm. No, not something. *Someone.*

"Melissa, it's ok!"

I still, breathing heavily, and open my eyes that I hadn't realized were shut and see a deer running across the path and back into the woods.

"*Ohhh . . .*" I breathe, smiling a bit. "It's just a deer."

"She's a pretty one," Sam comments.

He lets go of my arm and walks in the direction of the shrubs where the deer just emerged. I was going to ask where he was going, but I didn't want to be "shooshed" again because I am sure I would have to slap him at that point. So, I just follow him. We walk past the shrub, deeper into the forest—away from the path—and suddenly we both stop. My eyes widen at the sight before me.

"It's a . . . cabin?" I utter, my heartbeat picking up pace again. *Someone lives here??*

I nervously back up a few steps, but Sam moves forward. I watch as he approaches the cabin, glancing around. I'm rooted to my spot, wondering many things. *Why is there a cabin in the middle of the woods? Who owns it? Do they live here now? Whose land is this? What are we doing here? RUN!*

"Melissa, it's ok," Sam says as if sensing my unease. My anxiety must be oozing through my pores. "I think it's abandoned."

I force a smile and cautiously step forward, twigs and leaves crunching under my sneakers as I make my way to where Sam stands in front of the structure. The cabin is small—the size of a shed, really—with a flat sheet of tin as a roof. It looks like someone just tossed it onto the wooden structure. The wood of the cabin is old and looks rotten in many places. I'm surprised this building is still standing, though it does seem to be leaning a bit. There's a window on either side of a wood door that looks like it's hanging off the hinges. Both windows are broken. I notice a rusty wheelbarrow on the side of the cabin and a rake leaning against it. It's all so strange.

"Amazing," Sam mutters.

I wonder if he's drumming up a book idea in his mind. Although, I think this would make a better murder mystery than paranormal. I shudder a little at the thought, wondering why my mind always goes to those dark places.

"Should we go in?" I whisper.

Sam shrugs, looking at me. "I mean, we can see if the door is open. I doubt it has a lock on it, being way out here."

I nod and we carefully step up to the door. Sam puts his hand around the wooden knob and turns it, then pushes the door. It opens.

Sam turns to grin at me, then steps inside, and with wide eyes, I follow. My eyes take a second to adjust to the darkness, but once they do, I see the cabin is simply one room. There's no furniture, but a few crates are stacked on one end, a shovel and bucket sit against another wall, and rusted cans are scattered about. It looks so sketchy, like someone used it to hide out temporarily. The empty room is cold and mysterious. I shiver a little and turn to Sam.

"Well, it's not exactly cozy," Sam says, and I wonder if he's trying to make a joke. His head turns as he looks around and I see something in his eyes—something I can't make out. He almost doesn't look like himself. Or, rather, the "him" that I've known since I met him.

"Ok, well, let's get out of here. It's kind of spooky." I start walking toward the door and hear Sam chuckle.

"Ah, come on, Melissa. You're not scared, are you?"

"No, I just don't think—"

"I thought you were the brave one."

My head snaps around so fast I think my neck might snap. I narrow my eyes at Sam. "What did you say?"

He walks toward me, stopping about a foot away. "I said, I thought you were the brave one." His eyes narrow as he gazes into mine.

My eyes widen, and we stand there, staring at each other. Fear creeps in, and I suddenly get a chill and take a step back. I need to get out of here. It's not safe. Why isn't it safe? Is *Sam* not safe?

"I thought you were the brave one." I've heard that before.

I don't know Sam hardly at all other than the fact that he's been a nice neighbor. Now I'm in the woods alone with him—somewhere so far out that he could murder me and no one would know. Who would know?

"Come on, Lis—I mean, Melissa. I'm joking." Sam pats me lightly on the arm, then pushes past me and heads out the door.

Joking? Well, the man has as dark sense of humor then.

I take a shuddering breath and follow, not bothering to close the door.

Sam is walking back toward the path, so I follow, eager to get away from that cabin. At least I'm walking behind him. I'd hate for him to be walking behind me, able to attack if he wanted to. I stuff my hands inside my pockets and put my head down as I walk, hundreds of thoughts whirling inside my brain. My head is beginning to ache, and I fear I may have another memory coming. I sure hope I don't black out.

As I walk toward the path, I can't help but glance back at the dilapidating structure, and my mind can't stop playing the words that Sam said to me.

"I thought you were the brave one."

CHAPTER 15

SAM AND I arrive back at my house in the late afternoon, and he heads to his house. I don't bother inviting him in for coffee because my head is pounding and I'd feel safer alone. That notion makes me want to laugh a little. Never thought I'd feel that way.

After taking a hot shower and changing into lounge pants and a long-sleeve tee, I grab my journal and head outside. The weather is perfect—warm enough to be comfortable with a slight breeze. I sit there and listen to the familiar country sounds I've been getting used to. The cornstalks sway slightly with the breeze, almost as if they are dancing to celebrate the end of summer. A few drivers zoom past my house and wave at me. I don't recognize any of them, but I figure they are either being friendly or recognize me from around town.

I finally open my journal, ready to write. I've been journaling for several years now, at the suggestion of my therapist, to help trigger some memories of my early childhood. So far, it hasn't been very helpful. In my entry, I write about coming home, meeting Sam, exploring some old barns, and the cabin in the woods.

The cabin.

Sam seemed to know where he was going when we followed that trail. Has he been down there since he moved in the house across the road? I glance up and don't see anyone in the windows at his house, but I have a chilling sense that someone is watching. I quickly look back at my journal.

Sam's words echo in my head. *"I thought you were the brave one."* Where have I heard those words before? For some reason, it triggers a pounding heartbeat and a throbbing headache as memories try to resurface. *Who said that to me?* I hardly think I'm brave now, but maybe I was when I was little.

Suddenly, a screeching bird's cry breaks my concentration and startles me. Now, I don't mind birds and their little chirping, but these screeching birds are getting on my very last nerve.

I look up and see that it is getting cloudy, the air cooling just a little. I don't think I'll stay here forever. I mean, everything is paid for, thanks to my father renting the cornfields to put away money in a trust for me when I got older, but I will have to get a job at some point, and this house . . . well, this house creeps me out. It seems ominous. Dark. Like so many secrets reside here.

Dr. Hansen hadn't wanted me to leave, and though the thought of being safe—I *had* felt safe there—I still felt like I was being kept a prisoner. Home, facility, or whatever you want to call it, it's still the same thing: a place where I was kept safe both from the outside world and my own thoughts.

"Why can't my parents tell you what happened? Why do I have to remember?"

"Melissa, you must unlock the details of your time on the farm. Your parents simply cannot do that for you. You were in—well, you were in shock when you woke from your coma. You weren't right for months. Your parents do not even know the details of what happened. All they know is—"

Dr. Hansen stopped speaking when his phone rang. He said it was urgent and hurried out of the room, leaving a small, confused little girl to wonder what, exactly, her parents knew.

I shake my head at the memory of that time with Dr. Hansen. We never came around to what my parents knew. It never came up, and I learned not to bring it up anymore.

I write a little more in my journal and come up with an idea. Rachel and Megan—the two young women I met my second day here. Rachel said we went to school together. Megan seemed like she knew something. Something about my past? Surely they must know what happened to me back then. Kids don't just up and leave school for no reason. But Rachel seemed to close up when it came to mention of my neighbors. So, I'm going to have to try to get through to Megan. And I'll do that soon.

That decided, I take my journal and head inside for the evening.

*****

I wake the next morning to a cloudy sky but thankfully no rain. Yet. It's after eight, so I make coffee and put some waffles in the toaster. I plan on walking up the road to ask Rachel where Megan lives so I can chat with her, but I don't want to go too early. I also don't want to get caught in the rain, and it does look like rain will come at some point.

I eat quickly and take a cup of coffee outside. Despite the clouds and chilly morning air, the birds are in the trees, chirping away. I'll have to see if I can put up some sort of bird feeder. Won't hurt to feed them while I'm here. I wonder if there are any deer in the fields or even in my yard. I don't remember seeing any near the house when I lived here way back when, but that doesn't mean they didn't appear on occasion.

As I sip my coffee, I subtly glance across the road. The house looks dark, the curtains closed. Sam is a strange fellow, but he's been kind to me. I am torn between wanting to trust him and wanting to keep him at arm's length. First, I don't want to become too close only for him to leave someday. It would hurt to lose a friendship and be completely alone here again. Plus, he's said some weird things and makes me feel uneasy at times. Maybe he's not an open book like some people. I'm probably just not used to being around people in the "real world" to be able to tell the difference. I wonder if I ought to go to town more, try to get involved in some community stuff to make friends. Then again, I still don't know if I want to stay here long-term. And what would I do around here? Go to church? Hang out at one of the many bars? Options are limited here.

I finally go inside and get dressed, then head out to walk up the road. An occasional dog's bark can be heard in the neighborhood. Other than that, it's a quiet morning—no kids playing outside today. It *is* Sunday; maybe everyone is at church.

I stop walking.

"Melissa, let's go! We're going to be late for church!"

I ignored my mother's pleas. I wanted to finish one more chapter of my book. Jeff and I agreed we'd finish by Saturday night so we could talk about it on Sunday after church. The grown-ups always talked too long after church, so Jeff and I hung around playing in the dirt (then got yelled at by our parents) or talking about the books we'd just read. We were reading The Fisherman's Wife together.

"Melissa!"

"Coming!"

One more paragraph. One more paragraph.

"You have thirty seconds, young lady!"

Uh oh; that was Papa calling. Shoot. One more paragraph, and then . . . DONE!

I ran downstairs and out the door before I could get scolded. As we rode to church, I had a smile on my face. I couldn't wait to tell Jeff my thoughts about the last few chapters.

Jeff again, invading my memories. My head hurts now, and I feel sick to my stomach, so I turn around and hurry back to my house. All I want to do is get some water and lie on the couch.

I reach my house in record time and push the porch

door to open, but it slams into something, startling me. I push again. It's stuck!

What in the world . . .?

There's no fear, just anger, so I kick the door and hear a crash. When I look down, I see a large plastic tub with the word CHLORINE on it laying on its side, with two paint cans next to it. I glance around frantically, wondering who did this. My eyes land on Sam's house across the road and I frown. *Is he playing tricks on me? Are there kids on this road who are playing tricks on me? The "crazy lady" who came back to the farm? That's ridiculous, though.*

I kick the bucket and paint cans out of my way and storm into the house, grab a bottle of water, and plop down on the couch, not closing the door.

What the hell is going on?

* * * * *

Later that afternoon, I'm looking through some papers I found in a box in the hallway—the plastic tub and paint cans I found on the front porch earlier long forgotten—when I hear a knock at my door. I look up, expecting Sam to be standing there. Maybe he can shed some light on the porch incident. If he noticed someone over here, that would be helpful. Then I could call the police and not worry about them thinking I'm nuts.

It's Megan. She's alone and wearing a tentative smile,

her hands stuffed into a pair of worn jeans. I gesture for her to come in. As she does, she glances around.

"I'm sorry to just drop by," she tells me, not seeming nervous at all. I feel glad that she is comfortable around me. It's a shift from how her sister Rachel acts.

"Anytime. Really," I assure her. "It gets so lonely here. In fact, I've been wanting to talk to you. Want some coffee or water?"

"Oh, no, thank you. I just wanted to see how you're settling in. Ask if you need anything."

We sit down, and I wrinkle my nose at my cold coffee. I wonder how long it has been sitting there.

"Rachel told me you stopped over."

"Oh. Yes. I was taking a walk, and . . ." I am stammering, I know that. But I'm not sure what to say next. Should I prod Megan for answers? Should I ask her the same questions I asked Rachel? She definitely has a more open personality.

"Can I ask you something?" Megan says suddenly.

"Sure." I'm a bit taken aback at her abruptness, but I let her go on.

"Well, see, um . . . When we were kids, we were told that you went to an . . . *institution*." The last word is said in a whisper.

My eyes widen and I gasp. I wasn't aware that anyone knew where I went. I quickly clear my throat, trying to recover from shock when I notice Megan's blush.

"I'm sorry," she says quickly. "I had no right to ask. It's just . . ." She shrugs and smiles sheepishly.

I understand then. She was young when I went away. I'm sure there were plenty of others who wanted to know what happened to me—if the rumors were true. I, however, have nothing to hide. So, I tell the truth.

"Well, I know I was in a coma for a while." Megan gasps, and I shrug. "I don't know why or what happened. After treatments, I was allowed to go home. Here. But I don't remember that time. I was told that my parents brought me back, but after a week, I was put in a facility. They couldn't handle me here. I couldn't handle being here. I wouldn't even go outside. But I had no idea why."

"That sounds awful," Megan says, shaking her head. "I didn't realize."

"I was then put in a place we called "the house," which was really a place for me to get physical therapy, counseling, and get myself together so I could be on my own someday."

Megan's brows furrow. "You had an accident. I heard that."

I sit up, wanting to know more. "Yes. But no one will tell me what happened. My therapist said I need to remember on my own. Something about triggers and it would be worse if I was told rather than remembering. My parents never wanted to talk about it. But it's so frustrating!"

Megan nods and smiles almost sadly. "Strange that your parents wouldn't have told you anything. And what about Jeff?"

"Jeff?" *The kid in the picture I drew? The one who haunts my memories?*

"Hello!"

Megan and I both startle at the voice. We turn and see Rachel standing there, her eyebrows raised as if she is amused, and I wonder what the exchange is about. I'm sure they've talked about me—not just as kids but in the present since I returned. I shrug it off. I could care less what they think of me. They're simply keys to revealing some of my past. I am disappointed that she has just shown up, though. I never seem to get Megan alone so we can properly talk.

"Rach!" Megan jumps up and gives her sister a hug. "I'm sorry; I forgot about our appointment!"

"That's ok." Rachel smiles and looks at me. "Sorry, I must steal this one."

I stand and nod, sorry that I can't continue my conversation with Megan.

Megan waves before heading out with her sister. "Let's get together again soon, ok?"

"Wait, I—"

Megan is out the door before I can finish. I stand there and watch them happily trot off.

CHAPTER 16

"MELISSA . . . HELP . . . ME . . ."

I wake with a start, drenched in sweat. *Who said that?* I heard . . . I heard a voice. *Didn't I?* It's dark still. I lean over and glance at the alarm clock. 3:05 a.m. *Why did I wake up? Bad dream?* I shiver and sit up in bed, my eyes adjusting to the dark room. The moon gives enough light outside to lend a little light through the windows. I leave the curtains open when I sleep. There's nothing outside except the backyard and barns; I have nothing to worry about leaving the curtains open.

I sigh and lie back down. Now I'm restless, but I know I must get some sleep. My eyes are closing as I feel myself surrendering to sleep when I hear a clanging sound. I bolt up and look around. It sounded like it was outside, so I peek out the window. *Is that a shadow? Is someone out there? An animal? A human?* The shadow moves and I watch it. *It looks like a person!*

I jump up and grab the baseball bat I keep near my bed, then run downstairs so I can go outside and check it out. I know it's dumb to go out of the house in the country early in the morning while everyone sleeps and I'm all alone, but I do have a baseball bat, and I am getting tired of wondering if someone is sneaking around the property. It's not like the police will do anything about it.

I pull on a coat and slip my feet into some boots, then grab a flashlight and head out the door. I don't even try to be quiet about it or shut the door behind me. Fear turns into anger, and I'm so fed up at this point I'm ready for anything. I'm beginning to hate this place. Out in the middle of nowhere, surrounded by cornfields and elusive memories. Surrounded by people who say strange things or won't say anything, like everything is a damn mystery. Fed up doesn't begin to describe how I feel.

I step into the early morning air and breathe in. Cool and crisp. My eyes dart around. Across the street, there are no lights on. The road is dark, naturally, and nothing seems to lurk around the yard to my right. I glance to my left. The cornfield.

I hear coyote something suddenly. A rustling noise. I squint to see better but it's dark. A howls in the distance. A neighborhood dog barks in response. I shiver and pull my coat closer around my body, then slowly make my way toward the cornfield. My mind suddenly flits to a book I read not too long ago—a murder mystery about a young woman who was being stalked. She walked right into the killer's lair by being stupid, not paying attention to her surroundings. So I stop and look down toward the barns and back at the cornfield. *What am I doing?* I shouldn't walk into a trap; I need to be inside, secure and safe. Which is a joke since the house has no locks on any of the doors. Ideally, I'd call the cops, but I'm not about to be made a fool of again.

I turn back to my house when I get the urge to look across the road again. The lights in the house are still off, but there's someone standing in the yard.

Sam?

I gasp and hurry into my house, then push a chair under the door handle. A character in one of the books I read once did that so the perpetrator couldn't get in. I hope it works if someone is after me!

I go into the living room and peek through the curtains. Whoever I saw standing in the yard across the street isn't there anymore.

They are standing on my front lawn.

I scream and run upstairs into my room and crawl into my bed. I'm shaking from head to toe.

What the hell is going on in this house? Is someone stalking me? Is Sam . . . No, why would he want to harm me? Then again, he is a stranger. *A murderer, perhaps?* Could be. Says he's a writer, keeps to himself, acts like a weirdo sometimes . . .

Maybe I should suck it up and call the cops again. No; they'll just think I'm crazy. Besides, Giganto already warned me that I should get a lock for the front door. Perhaps I will after this.

I listen for sounds, just anything that would signal approaching footsteps. If someone is really out there, I need to be ready to protect myself. I clutch my bat tightly as I listen to the night, but I don't hear anything. Still, I must stay awake.

*****

The sun is streaming through my window, and I blink a few times. Thank goodness I fell asleep after the awful morning I went through. I pull on a pair of leggings and an oversized shirt, slip my flip flops on, and head downstairs. I set to make the coffee, and a glance at the clock tells me it's after nine. *Goodness, but I slept in!*

I look out the window, so many thoughts running

through my mind but so fuzzy from broken sleep. There's no one out there. *Of course there isn't.*

I'm not hungry, so when the coffee is ready, I pour a mug and sit at the table with my journal, recapping events of late. I can barely concentrate. Loneliness and despair overcome me. I was a fool to come back here. Well, alone anyway. But I had no one else. My parents are dead and my grandmother in a home. I'm alone. *How long will I be alone?*

I can't sit here anymore. I get up and head to the room above the kitchen. I hate these stairs. They're steep and treacherous, no carpet. I make it upstairs without killing myself and walk to the room I haven't looked in yet. What will I find behind the door? I reach for the handle and turn it, thinking the door will open easily, but it seems stuck. I shove my body against it, and it finally opens. I regain my balance and realize I'm standing in another bedroom. I'm confused, though. I know where my parents' bedroom is. I know where mine is. It must have been my grandma's when she lived here. I try to conjure up memories, but nothing comes. I seriously do not remember this room.

There's a worn brown carpet and light blue walls. A window is on one wall, a slanted ceiling on another. There's a twin bed and a small nightstand with a lamp sitting on top. A small dresser sits against one wall, and a couple large boxes are next to it.

Then I notice another door. A closet maybe? I am not about to look in there. Right now, I feel it's pointless. I looked into this room to find a bedroom, but now I'm done. Maybe I can explore further at another time, but right now, I'm satisfied knowing it's just a bedroom. No secrets, no ghosts. Just a bedroom.

I step out, close the door, and head back downstairs, feeling like I'm no closer to answers even though I've explored nearly every room in this damn house.

CHAPTER 17

I AM WAITING for some frozen chicken tenders and french fries to cook in the oven when I hear a soft knock on the door. I grab the baseball bat that's leaning against the cupboard, just in case. It's nearly dark, and I'm sure it's not any of the people looking to buy my dad's old junk in the barn. Besides, given all of the strange happenings lately, I am not taking any chances.

I open the door to see Megan standing there, wearing jeans and a long-sleeve shirt, her hair in a ponytail. She looks so casual and relaxed. I immediately smile and invite her to come in. She steps into the kitchen.

"Sorry to just drop in."

"Are you kidding? I'm just waiting for my pathetic

dinner. I welcome the company!"

Her face changes suddenly, and I'm stunned for a moment until I realize why she's making a face.

"Ah, the food!" I cry as I hurry to open the oven and pull the cookie sheet out. Thankfully, nothing is burned.

Megan laughs and says, "I'm a terrible cook. Rachel is the cook in our family. I live on this stuff. Doesn't look too bad, though."

"Well then, join me, will you?"

I put the food on a platter and pull out a couple of paper plates. Then I open the refrigerator and grab a bottle of Pinot Grigio and hold it out.

"Wine?"

"Of course! Thank you."

Megan sits at the table, and I grab two wine glasses and pour. After setting out ketchup and barbecue sauce for dipping, we dig into the food. Everything is very crispy, but not burned, so it tastes good. Megan and I eat and sip our wine while having casual conversation. I feel so relaxed, so *normal* around her—like we've been friends forever. She's definitely the more relaxed and fun of the two sisters. *No offense, Rachel,* I think.

"Megan," I say, finishing off a french fry. "Why does Rachel seem so reserved when I ask about my past? Is it some big secret? Something I should know about?"

Megan sets her glass down and looks at me for a moment. "You must understand that Rachel acts much older than her age. We always joked that she was the "old lady" of the family. Most like my mother in that respect." She chuckles and wipes her hand on a napkin, seeming to think before continuing. "We were brought up to keep to ourselves and not get into anyone else's business, not to gossip, stuff like that. When you left, people were hush-hush about it. We never understood why. And Rachel followed our mother's lead and keeps a tight lid on anything she does know." She shrugs and sits back.

I sit back and ponder what I've just heard. Clearly, my past can't be anything shameful. Nothing so bad happened that people have to keep hush about it, right?

"Look," she says, gulping down the rest of her wine. "The past is the past. No use dredging it up."

I nod and finish my own wine, even though I don't agree with her. I must know what happened, now that I'm back and weird things keep happening. It's almost like the past is haunting me on purpose—to be found out. I still don't completely understand. I mean, there was an accident, I was in the hospital, Jeff and his parents moved, and that's that.

But there must be more than that . . .

I decide to let it go for now. We finish eating and clean up, then I pour us each another glass of wine and suggest we sit in the living room, where it's more comfortable. Megan sits on the couch and curls her legs under her. I sit on the recliner.

"Do you use that?" Megan asks, pointing to the woodstove.

I shake my head as I swallow some wine. "Not yet. I'd like to. I think I need to get it cleaned or looked at first." I suppress a shudder, remembering the sight of the wood being there and then not.

"*Sooooo* . . . What do you know of your neighbor. Sam, right? He's kind of cute." Megan wiggles her eyebrows a little, and I almost spit my wine out laughing.

"Yes, he is, but I am certainly not thinking of him like that. Or anyone. You're welcome to him." I look off into the distance thinking that I've never thought of any man like that. I've been so busy trying to get my life together and then coming here . . .

"Don't mind if I do, then," Megan says.

This time, I *do* spit out the wine I just took a sip of. I start laughing and Megan joins in. When we calm down, Megan turns serious.

"Really, though. I mean, you're in this house all alone with only a single guy across the road. The next nearest neighbor is up the road a bit. And Rachel and I are even farther up. Do you feel safe?"

I shrug. "Well, there have been some weird things happening. And it's a little spooky being alone. But Sam has been nice. I've no reason not to trust him." *I don't think.*

Megan stands up and walks over to the window, parting the curtains a little. "Doesn't look like he's home."

"Maybe he went to town. Or is sleeping?" I suggest, not caring one way or another.

Megan turns to me. "Yeah, right. It's, like, a little after seven."

I stand, and she holds up her near-empty glass. I smile. I'm all for us having a little more wine together. I've been enjoying her company so much I don't want her to leave! It's been so long since . . . Well, it's been *never* since I had someone to chat with and giggle over things. You know, like real friends.

We walk into the kitchen, and I top off our glasses.

"Let's go outside," Megan says, heading out the door.

I follow her and am pleasantly surprised that the evening is only slightly cool. Everything seems so calm. And quiet. Almost eerily quiet. The sun is starting to set; a gentle breeze pushes the corn stalks to sway gently, and the scene is eerie, almost mesmerizing. Beyond the fields are rolling hills, with windmills lined up at the top of them.

We sit at the table and sip our wine in silence. Megan slips her shoes off and tucks her feet under her. I love that she's so relaxed around me. I glance across the road to Sam's house, wondering if he is home. And wondering why I now care.

"You know," I say, finding myself about to let loose to Megan because I need the friendship, and the wine is loosening my tongue. "I've been over there."

"You have?" Megan's eyes widen.

"Sam asked me over for tea one evening, and I—"

"Whoa! You went over to his house? *Alone?* At night?"

"Oh, please. It was nothing. We had some tea and just chatted a bit."

"Tea?" Megan smirks. "So what did you talk about?" She glances over at the house as she gulps down some more wine. *Goodness, this girl will be buzzed before I know it.*

"Actually, he was asking questions about the house. Seems very interested in it."

"*His* house?"

"*My* house."

We sit in silence for a minute, each in our own thoughts. A coy dog howls in the distance. Or is it a coyote? I'm not even sure what's out here. I wish I had grown up here instead of leaving at a young age. This seems like a great place to grow up. The barns, the house, the cornfields . . .

"Tag, you're it!"

"Hey, don't run so fast!"

I giggled as he sprinted through the cornfield, ignoring the painful jabs of the pointy stalks. It was fun running from him; he was so slow!

"I give up! Where are you?"

"Come and find me."

I sat down in the dirt, waiting for him to find me. He won't, of course, but it was fun listening to him try—the rustling of the cornstalks, the vastness of it all just for me. I could stay out here for such a long time. No one would ever find me.

"Are you ok?"

I blink as my mind registers Megan's words. Apparently, I had gone back to a memory. How long had I blanked out?

I clear my throat a little, then suck down the rest of my wine. "I did see something I thought was a little odd," I say, trying to take the attention off myself.

"What?"

I proceed to tell Megan about the room with the toys and boxes and the sliding glass door. "It was just strange," I confide. "Like, why is that stuff still there? And why doesn't Sam get rid of it?"

Megan stands abruptly and sets her now empty glass

down. "Let's go!"

"Huh?"

"Let's go over there and take a look." She is whispering now, as if someone is nearby. "Sam isn't home; that's obvious. I want to see what's in that room."

I stand now and put my hands on my hips. "Megan, we can't just break in."

"No, no. We won't. We'll just peek in the windows. Come on!"

Megan starts walking toward the road, and I stumble after her, almost wanting to giggle a little. I feel a good buzz from the wine now, and it's almost thrilling to be doing this—something almost . . . naughty.

I catch up with Megan, and instead of going to the driveway, she goes to the ditch and climbs up into the yard.

"This way," she whispers and hurries across the yard, past the large maple tree and toward the back of the house.

I hurry to catch up, almost giggling with disbelief, and we stop at the side of the house. Still no noise. No people. Megan grabs my hand and pulls me along. We creep to the back of the house, where we find a door and two concrete steps leading to it—the door to the strange room!

"Now what?" I whisper, still wanting to giggle. *Damn wine.*

Megan grins at me, then goes up the steps to the door.

She's peering in, and I come up behind her. We can't see a thing. It's dark. To my surprise and horror, Megan reaches for the door handle. I quickly place my hand on hers.

"We cannot break in."

"It's not breaking in if it's unlocked," she whispers a bit too loudly.

I shake my head but let her go. She turns the handle, and to our surprise, the door opens. Megan grins at me, and I peer over her shoulder.

At first, there's nothing to see, it's too dark. Then . . .

Megan jumps back and we stumble off the steps, landing in a pile on the back lawn.

"What the heck?" I cry.

"Sam . . ." Megan starts, and I see she's shaking.

I stand up, wiping my hands on my jeans. "Sam *what?*" I hiss.

"He's . . . He's there."

I roll my eyes. Megan must actually be drunk. I go back up the steps and open the door, this time not bothering to be discreet. Then I gasp and step back, stumbling off the steps once again.

"What?" she cries.

"Run!"

I pull Megan up, and we take off running across the

lawn toward the ditch.

CHAPTER 18

WE JUMP DOWN into the ditch and run across the road to my house and into the kitchen. I slam the door shut and grab the wine bottle, grabbing new glasses from the cupboard since ours are outside, and I'm not about to go out there.

We greedily gulp down some wine and stare at each other, panting, trying to catch our breath.

"Did you see?" Megan asks.

"Sam. I saw . . ." I'm not even able to finish.

"Sam," she whispers.

We head to the living room with our glasses. Megan curls up on the couch and pulls a blanket over her body. I plop down in the recliner and grab another blanket, pulling it over my shoulders. We drink our wine in the dim room and continue looking at each other, both of us at a loss for words. What we both saw was a near dark room full of boxes and toys, and Sam crouched in the corner, his knees pulled up to his chest, his head on his knees.

And he was crying.

"Melissa?"

"Yeah?"

"What did we see?"

I sit back on the recliner, pulling the blanket tighter around my shoulders. "I don't know." And it's true. I *don't* know. We are both well under the influence of alcohol and scared out of our wits. Did we really see Sam in the dark, crying in a corner? Or was it our overactive and alcohol-induced imaginations?

Megan sets her glass on the stand next to the couch, then flops herself down and closes her eyes. I close my eyes, still gripping my wine glass. Megan can spend the night here since it's late. I don't mind one bit. I'm pretty freaked out and shaken up.

Megan eventually falls asleep, and I listen to her steady breathing. I don't sleep much, as dreams invade my mind, and as the hours crawl by, it gets brighter outside, so I quietly get up and go to the kitchen to set about making coffee. After setting the pot to perk and taking a quick glance into the living room to make sure Megan is still sleeping, I slip on a pair of sneakers and step outside.

The air is crisp, and there is dew on the grass. The birds are awake and chattering, no doubt waiting for food. I decide I definitely want to start feeding the birds. There are bird feeders around the property, so my mother must have fed them once upon a time.

I walk around the house, not really sure what—if anything—I'm looking for. It's just dawn, and the world seems asleep. I should be asleep. After walking back to the front, my shoes squishing in the grass, my head involuntarily turns to the right toward Sam's house. No lights. No person. Just . . . stillness.

I heave a sigh and go back to the kitchen, where Megan sits, holding a mug of coffee. Her hair is wild around her face and she looks like she didn't sleep at all, though I know she did.

"Hey," she says when I walk in.

"Get much sleep?" I pour myself a full mug of coffee and plop down in a chair next to Megan.

She yawns and shakes her head. "A little. I'll head home and try to sleep for an hour, then I have to work at ten."

"Where do you work?"

"I work from home doing data entry. Twenty-eight

bucks an hour for part-time. Not too shabby." She sips her coffee and grimaces.

I laugh at the face she makes. "Sorry. I like my coffee strong."

"Better than nothing," she mumbles.

I can't get my mind off last night—what we did, what we saw. I figure we should talk about it.

"Megan, do you suppose—"

I'm cut off by a loud knock on the door. We both jump and look at each other with wide eyes. Who would be coming over at this hour? It's barely six!

The knock again. Megan shakes her head, but curiosity gets the best of me. Besides, people don't murder people when it's daylight . . . right?

I open the door and startle a little when I see Sam standing there. This is not the same man we saw—or thought we saw—last night. This man here is wearing dress pants and a button-down shirt with shiny dress shoes, his hair gelled back, and he's smiling. He looks . . . normal.

"Good morning. Forgive me for stopping over so early. I—" He stops suddenly, noticing Megan, and I swear I saw something like annoyance flash in his eyes. But it was over before I could figure out if it was there or my imagination. "Oh, hello."

Megan nods and stands. I shift uncomfortably on my

feet.

Sam recovers quickly and smiles again. "I was just wondering, Melissa, if you saw or heard anything . . . *strange* last night."

My eyebrows raise, and I glance at Megan, who shrugs. I notice she's backed away from her chair and is standing close to the counter where I keep the butcher knives.

"Strange. Like . . ."

Sam shrugs his shoulder. "It's probably nothing. You see, I was working in my office last night and heard some noises outside. I looked around but didn't see anything. Still, I wanted to check with you. You never know up here in the middle of nowhere who could be lurking around unwanted. Uninvited."

Nobody says anything for what seems like minutes. I finally clear my throat and shake my head. "We were here. We didn't see anything." I look to Megan, who nods in agreement.

"Hmm. Ok."

Sam turns to leave, and I let out a breath I didn't realize I was holding. Then he turns around.

"Sometimes, we see things that are not there. Do you understand what I'm saying?" His eyes are dark as they focus on me, and they don't look normal for a moment—

like the chaos you'd see in a mad man's eyes.

I don't know how to respond, so I just say, "Um, ok. What do you mean?"

I take a step back, creating more distance between us. Sam is strange, but lately I've been wondering if he knows more than he lets on. Just like how he knew I abruptly left this house when I was a kid even though I hadn't mentioned it. Or maybe he's the one causing weird things to happen around here. I shake that thought off as quickly as it comes. What would he have to gain by that?

"Just . . . be careful. Ok?" He says this, and I nod once, trying to act as normally as possible. "I'll see you around." He turns around to leave, not bothering to acknowledge Megan.

"What. The. Hell."

I turn at the sound of Megan's voice. I'm thinking the same thing.

"Do you think he knows?" she hisses, peeking out the window next to the door, no doubt checking to see if Sam has indeed left. She turns back to me and crosses her arms over her chest.

"No idea. I mean, he was awfully weird about it. We did see him, right? It was . . . him?"

Megan shakes her head. "Don't know. Had to be, though."

I start laughing suddenly—whether from exhaustion or losing my mind a little, I'm not sure. "You know what? We had fun visiting last night, had too much wine, decided to peek in my neighbor's house, thought we saw something, and now we think everything is basically out of a murder mystery book."

Megan is looking at me like I've lost it. And maybe I have. Still, I give her an *Aren't I right?* look.

"Geez, Melissa!" she cries, throwing her hands in the air. "I think there's something odd going on with your neighbor, and I think we should find out. Forget the fact that he's good-looking. Psychos and serial killers are not all gross-looking."

"We're not detectives! And this is dangerous."

She blows out her breath in frustration. "One minute you're wary of living here alone and maybe even a little scared, then the next minute, you're not. Which is it?"

I lean against the counter and sigh. I can't answer her question because I don't know the answer. All I know is that I'm tired. I'm confused. Maybe I'm even a little angry because I don't know whether Sam is a good guy or not.

Before I say anything, Megan steps up to me and places her hand on my arm. Her expression softens.

"Look, I have to go. We both need a little rest. We can

talk about this later."

I nod and follow Megan out the door. The morning is slightly warming up, and it makes me feel better. Maybe I can forget the Sam thing and the events of last night.

"Ok. We'll talk later," I say.

Megan waves as she walks away, and I watch her, willing my eyes not to rove across the road at Sam's house. I'm becoming obsessed with my neighbor.

CHAPTER 19

"HAVE YOU SEEN KRISTI?"

"Which one is Kristi?" he asked, his hands on his hips.

I knew he was impatient—we wanted to get to our tree fort to work on it before we had to go back to the house to have lunch. But I needed to find my doll first.

"You know Kristi! She has dimples on her cheeks!" I huffed out. Boys are dumb. They don't remember things like your favorite doll. They only worry about their silly GI Joe toys.

He rolled his eyes. "We can't bring her. Your mom will get mad. She'll get dirty!"

"I don't want to bring her. I just want to make sure I know where she is."

"Lissy," he started, but I put on my best pouty face because I

knew he'd give in. "Ok," he said softly. "Let's find Kristi." He took my hand, and we went inside the house to find my favorite doll.

* * * * *

I open my eyes in the morning to a cloudy sky, but birds are chirping, so it can't be that bad. Then again, what do I know about birds and weather?

I lie there for a minute, my mind going back to the dream I had. *Kristi.* That was the name of my doll. Could that be the same doll I found in the chicken coop? Sam told me he had a cousin who had a doll named Kristi. Seems like an odd coincidence.

I shake my head and stretch, taking my time getting out of bed, then dress in an old pair of jeans and oversized T-shirt. I plan on going through more of the playroom today to see what other things I can find . . . and throw away.

As I walk down the stairs, I glance around and am dismayed at all of the boxes and junk I hadn't really paid attention to before. But I swear I cleared out most of the boxes down here some days ago.

When I reach the bottom step, my gaze falls on more dusty boxes. They look like they want to be discovered, what with the way papers are sticking out. Some possibilities keep flitting through my mind: one, this house is somehow alive and moving things; two, there's a ghost running around. A third possibility would be that I'm losing my mind, and I won't easily dismiss that.

Still, I'm confused as I try to recall noticing the boxes before, but the longer I stare, the more convinced I am that there's someone who keeps coming into my home unwanted.

With furrowed brows, I approach the boxes, and something causes me to hesitate for a moment before tentatively reaching out to touch them. It's as if I'm expecting them to vanish into thin air, but they remain solid beneath my fingertips. I might as well go through them; maybe I'll find something helpful. Every time I set about finding clues that could trigger my memory and give me answers, I only end up more frustrated than I before. I can only manage snippets and flashes before the headaches take over.

Crouching down, I lift the lid of the topmost box and peer inside. I rummage through the forgotten stuff, shifting fading newspapers aside, already getting the feeling that this is another waste of time. I should be outside, checking out the barns. I've thought that so many times, but whenever I explore the barns, something strange always seems to happen. Maybe Megan can explore them with me.

My hands brush against something solid. Nestled among some newspapers is a weathered diary. I pull it out and slide my thumb across its yellow pages. I haven't found anything like it during my scavenging, and a hopeful bubble churns in my stomach. This could help me out.

I can't tell why my hands are trembling as I flip through the brittle pages, scanning the entries penned in faded ink. I run my hand over the words on one of the pages. From the elegant cursive, I know this belonged to my mother. Apart from the piano lessons, cursive writing was one of the other things she taught me as a kid. I know that because I've always known how to write in cursive. A couple of the women at the home where I grew up didn't know how to write in cursive. Their schools never taught them.

February 16
Today, Melissa had another one of her episodes. She claimed to see shadows moving in the corners of the room, but there was nothing there. I'm so scared for her.

My heart slams into my chest as I read that. I can't recall seeing things as a kid, but that could be because I can't actually remember much. However, the little that comes back is centered around the little boy—my best friend. Was Jeff an imaginary friend? *No, no, no, no.* I'm not crazy. Rachel and Megan can remember him. He was real! I squeeze my eyes shut, willing my apprehension to go away. I don't see things . . . shadows or whatever. Except for that figure I keep seeing in the dark, but there's no one else in this house to see it with me. I'm sure if I wasn't the only one cooped up here, I wouldn't be the only one noticing the strange things in this house.

I open my eyes and breathe out. I'm just going to read this and see where it goes. I can't calm the thumping in my chest, so I head to the kitchen, diary in hand. I quickly set to making coffee and pop some bread in the toaster. Then I read on.

February 20

I found her talking to herself again, whispering to someone who wasn't there. She becomes so lost in her own world whenever Jeff's not playing with her. I told Vincent that maybe she needed help but he says it's just kids' stuff. Children have imaginary friends all the time. I don't like this.

Jeff. Everything seems to be pointing to this one kid. At least I now know for sure that he was my best friend. And my neighbor. The nearest house to mine is the one where Sam is staying in, meaning that there's a high chance that that was Jeff's house. The more important question is:

Where is Jeff? I obviously left him behind after we moved out of here, but whatever happened to him? All of this runs through my mind as I butter my toast and take a bite, then pour my coffee and sit back down.

March 5

She keeps asking about her brother, but I don't have the heart to tell her the truth. It's been months since that terrible day, but the memory still haunts me. I can't bear to see the pain in her eyes when she asks, but it was an accident. She's just a child!

I don't feel anything. No memory is triggered, only the roaring noise that originates from somewhere in my head and now blurs my vision. Whatever reality I think I once had is threatening to mist away. *Brother? I've never had a brother; I'm an only child. What accident? Did I do something? Oh, I wish I could just get these answers!*

My heart is still thumping fast, but I refuse to acknowledge it. I know what's happening; I'm in denial of everything because nothing makes sense, and my head is throbbing along with my heartbeat, but I don't care. I'm not crazy. I never had a brother.

I run a hand through my hair in frustration, then sit back and finish my now-cold toast. I close my eyes and try to think. Nothing makes sense. I'm the only child of my parents. Even the old pictures hanging on the wall show just the three of us—my mom, my dad, and me. Not even my grandma. So what do the words in this diary mean?

I feel like my sanity is being threatened. What's the illusion? What's reality? Was it wise to come back here? Maybe I should've listened to my doctor and just moved on. But from what? I need to know who I was!

But I can't go back. I won't. I want my freedom. No matter what the cost.

I stretch and decide I will continue to go through boxes. I can do this. I will not lose my marbles over the past or stupid things that keep going on around here. If my sanity slips—even just a little—I'll be forced to go back.

Unless they don't find out. If I can hold it together just to stay here a little longer—long enough to finish cleaning it out and put it on the market—I can get my own apartment and leave this place behind once and for all. Maybe the smart thing to do would be to grab my belongings and leave now. Just go. But I don't think I can do that. Something is holding me here right now.

I finish my coffee and set the diary aside. There's nothing more. I'm still as confused as I had been—predictably so. Well, there's the new information that my mother thought I was a crazy child; she literally feared for me.

I walk over to the boxes and set the diary back where I found it and begin to stack the boxes against the wall. I will go through the rest later; I just don't want to right now.

I decide that later I will find some wood and try the woodstove. That will make it cozy also. Even though I know I should have the chimney checked and cleaned, I can't help it; I want a cozy fire. I deserve it. And so what if this whole house burns to the ground? Good riddance.

I walk back into the kitchen, and what I see sitting on the table next to the salt and pepper shakers is a doll—the doll that Sam called Kristi. It was not there when I was in the kitchen just moments ago.

The words from the diary come drifting back to me: *"She claims to see shadows moving . . ."*

"Melissa? Are you home?"

I jump out of my skin at the sudden sound of a voice. The doll is looking straight at me, as if observing my frayed nerves with satisfaction, so I walk away and whip open the front door. Sam is standing there, a concerned look on his face.

"Sam. What are you doing here?" I ask breathlessly, then realize I sounded rude. "Sorry. I mean—"

"It's ok." Sam holds a hand up and peers around me.

"Just stopping over to see if you want to go into town and get breakfast. My treat."

"Oh. Well . . . Ok, that's nice of you." I stand there stupidly for a moment. Should I go with him? I decide it is a good idea to get out of the house, and a free breakfast is certainly appealing. "Just let me get my sneakers on." It's not until now that I realize I am very hungry, not having had a proper breakfast.

"Take your time."

Is it really wise to have Sam around? I mean, he hasn't done anything wrong, but the mystery that drapes all over him is starting to make me feel uneasy. And what of the other night? What Megan and I saw. Too bad my now growling stomach takes over any reasoning in my head.

"No visitors today?" I know he's referring to Megan. He had seemed bothered by her the last time he saw her.

"Just me." I move out of the way, forgetting the stupid doll on the table, when I hear Sam chuckle. "What is she doing on the table?"

I yank my sneaker on one foot and grunt. "Oh, um, yeah, I set her up there so I wouldn't forget to put her in the giveaway pile."

"Really?" Sam picks up the doll and raises his eyebrows.

I finish getting my other sneaker on and stand up, taking

the doll from him. "You said your cousin had a doll like this. Kristi?"

"She did," he says softly. His eyes follow me as I set the doll on the chair at the farthest end of the table. "She loved that doll. Always wanted to make sure she was somewhere safe when she went somewhere and couldn't bring her."

I stand there, my body shaking, remembering the dream I had about me and some boy . . . and a doll named Kristi.

"You ready?" Sam's demeanor changes and he wears a smile.

"Sure. This ok to wear?" I gesture to my "work around the house" attire. Actually, it's become my everyday attire lately. I mean, it's not like I go anywhere.

Sam nods and we walk out of the house. His car is in front, still running, and I'm glad for that, since it's chilly. We climb into the car and take off to town, down the steep hill, past the farmhouses and fields.

"How's your book coming?" I try to make conversation, since the last time I saw Sam was when he appeared on my doorstep the day after Megan and I almost broke into his house.

He smiles. "Good. Very good. Being up here gives me just the inspiration I need."

"Mmm. Well, this place has all the creepy houses and weird-looking dolls; I'm sure you get plenty of inspiration just from my house."

He chuckles softly but doesn't say anything. I wonder if I should tell him about the diary, but I know I won't. It's too much to carry by yourself—these thoughts and things that make you question your sanity—but telling someone else about them is like an acknowledgment that you're delusional.

"Penny for those thoughts."

I look out the window as we drive past the houses and barns. I see a fenced-in green pasture dotted with cattle, unbothered by the light drizzling that has begun. If I had a camera, I would capture the scenery.

"Melissa?"

"Nothing. Just thinking about things I went through in the house."

He glances at me. "Did you find anything interesting?"

I don't want to think about the diary or the doll that materialized in the kitchen from nowhere.

"Just some old newspapers, that's all."

If he thinks I'm withholding anything, he says nothing about it, and we drive in silence until we pull up in front of a small building that has a neon sign saying EVA'S DINER above the wooden door. A few vehicles are parked in the small lot, and Sam parks beside a red Chevy truck.

"Hope you brought a big appetite with you."

I would laugh at that, but Sam looks like he's serious.

"Um, well . . . I would guess so?" How are you supposed to reply to a question like that?

"You look rather thin."

What?

Before I can react to what he said, Sam opens the door and steps out of the car. I climb out as well, noticing the drizzle has let up and the sun is just peeking out from behind some clouds. I follow closely behind, letting him lead the way in.

The diner is buzzing with low conversation as we settle into a cozy booth by the window. Sunlight streams through the curtains, casting a warm glow over the checkered tablecloth. How strange this weather is, going from drizzling rain to sunshine within minutes.

The waitress sets menus down in front of us and hurries off to get our coffee. I tuck a loose strand of hair behind my ear before scanning the laminated menu in front of me. I really should get my hair trimmed soon. It's long, past my shoulders, but probably appears straggly. I don't think I'd even know what a "modern-day" haircut would look like! I wonder if I can trim it myself. I really don't care about style right now. A ponytail will do just fine.

I decide I am going to order pancakes. "I haven't had

pancakes in a long while." I smile as a memory of me eating blueberry pancakes comes to mind. I think my mother told me I had a sweet tooth.

Sam chuckles, and his eyes crinkle with amusement—the first I've seen. "Then pancakes it is. You can't go wrong with a classic."

The waitress brings out two steaming mugs of coffee, and we place our order. As she walks away, I glance around, not being able to shake the feeling of being watched. There's nothing out of the ordinary—the usual mix of patrons enjoying their breakfast, the clatter of dishes in the kitchen, the soft murmur of conversation. Nothing odd. Then I notice a couple at a nearby table, their gaze lingering on me with an intensity that sends an involuntary shiver down my spine, and I quickly avert my eyes. I'm being paranoid.

"So, what are you calling your book?"

"No spoilers." Sam doesn't like talking about his book, and I find it strange, wondering if all writers are like this.

He doesn't smile, and that uneasy feeling I have about him returns. If I didn't have a lot to find out about myself, I'd like to find out who Sam is.

Just then, I remember that Sam is living in the house Jeff used to live in. Maybe he has seen something that could help me. It seems like things were left in that house when the previous owner left, given the state of the room I peeked into. Unless it's Sam's stuff, which would be extremely odd.

"You know, growing up, I used to have a best friend," I say, trying to broach the subject of the mysterious friend I had. Sam's eyes don't leave mine as I speak. "Jeff. He used to live where you're staying right now."

"Where's Jeff now?" Sam asks slowly.

I sigh. "Don't know. We, um, kind of lost track."

"Hmm," Sam says, looking over my head like he is thinking. "Maybe he didn't hang on long enough."

"What?"

Just then, our plates arrive, piled high with steaming pancakes and bacon, and my stomach rumbles in anticipation. Forgetting the odd thing Sam just said, I dig into my meal, not waiting for Sam, savoring each bite. Growing up, I had pretty good breakfasts, since some of my housemates were good cooks, but there's something about a greasy diner breakfast that is more satisfying than any breakfast cooked at home.

"Oh my God," I murmur, as if this is the first time I've ever tasted pancakes. They're cooked to perfection, and the sweet syrup clings to my tastebuds.

Sam smiles. But as I glance up from my plate, I catch

another fleeting glimpse of that couple watching me, their expressions unreadable. Nope, nothing's going to ruin my breakfast, imagination or not.

I eat in silence, and when I'm done, I realize I haven't felt such contentment ever since I came here—a refreshing break from the chaos that has followed me since waking from my coma.

"Excuse me."

I look up at hearing a small, delicate voice and see the couple sitting nearby now standing next to me. The man looks positively mortified, but the woman has a small smile on her face and wears almost a determined look. They're young, maybe early thirties if I had to guess. *Do I know them?*

I set my fork down and smile, hoping I don't have syrup on my face or anything. Sam looks at them curiously.

"We're sorry to disturb you. You're Melissa, right?" the woman says.

"I am. And you are . . . ?"

"Oh, forgive me. My name is Nancy, and this is my husband, Robert. We live on your road. Quite close, actually."

Oh! That's interesting. Maybe they've seen or heard something or even know me from long ago. I open my mouth to say something but am interrupted.

"I'm Sam, Melissa's neighbor. It's nice to meet you both." He says it with a guarded tone, almost challenging them to continue the conversation.

Nancy does not disappoint. "You see," she says while wringing her hands nervously, "I knew you when you were younger. I'm close to your age, but we were in different grades in school." She smiles brightly, but she's wringing her hands nervously. Her husband looks around like he's ready to flee.

"I'm sorry. I don't remember you. But it's nice to meet you both now," I say, trying to reassure them that it's ok they interrupted our breakfast. I was finished anyway.

Nancy nods. "Well, I was awfully sorry to hear about Jeff. So sad. But I heard he didn't—"

"Well," Sam cuts in, standing up. "It's so nice to meet you both, but we must be going."

Nancy looks startled, and I look at Sam in shock and annoyance. Nancy was going to say something—something that sounded important! Why did Sam rudely cut in?

Robert gently places his hand on Nancy's arm and she nods. They start to walk away, and she throws a glance over her shoulder. Something like a mixture of awe and fear. *What the hell?*

"I've got to do some work, Melissa."

I stand up and nod, still wondering what just happened.

It was incredibly rude how Sam interrupted. I'm about to say something to him about it, when I look down and notice Sam's plate—it's still full; he hasn't had a bite.

"Um, Sam?"

He looks up from his wallet where he's fishing out money to pay for breakfast.

"You didn't eat your pancakes," I comment, slightly embarrassed for mentioning it.

"Oh." He smiles and shoves his wallet back into his pocket. "I was lost in thought. Writer's mind, you know." He taps his head and grins. I *don't* understand but keep quiet. "I'll just take mine to go."

After the waitress boxes up his breakfast, we walk out, and I'm left wondering what Nancy was going to say about Jeff.

CHAPTER 20

BY THE TIME we get back to the house, the sun has disappeared behind the darkened clouds once again, and I don't know if it's going to rain. I say a quick goodbye to Sam before climbing out of the car, slamming the door shut, and running toward my house. I'm not giving him the chance to explain his rude behavior or make excuses for it. I've had enough of him for today, thank you. We didn't even talk the entire car ride back here. Maybe he had the sense to know I was fuming over his bad behavior at the diner.

I turn around before heading inside, but Sam's car is gone. Strange. He must have driven down the road. But that leads away from his house. Maybe he forgot something in town.

I shrug and hurry inside. As I put a pot of coffee on—diner coffee is decent but doesn't compare to the perked coffee I've become a pro at making—I think about that couple who approached our table and what Nancy had been about to say. It seems like every time I get close to hearing about something from my past, something or someone interrupts. This time, it had been Sam.

I shake my head and sigh, deciding nothing can be done about it now. It's not fair, really. To come that close to getting answers from an unlikely source only for the moment to be wrenched away. *Who is this mysterious Jeff, and what happened to him?* For a second, I wonder if Sam will tell me who he bought the house from. Maybe they are Jeff's parents or know what happened. But as quickly as the thought comes, I dismiss it. Sam seems very closed up when I bring things up. So instead, I decide that the next time I see Rachel or Megan, I'll ask them where Nancy and Robert live and perhaps pay them a visit. That is, if I remember to ask about them. My mind seems to remember and forget things quickly.

For now, I decide to look inside the desk that sits in the living room. I can't believe I haven't looked through that yet. No better time than today. Maybe later I'll try to scrounge up some wood for the woodstove.

While the coffee is perking, I go to the desk and sit on the chair. The desk is a sturdy oak that has a sole vintage brass lamp on it. I switch it on, happy to see the bulb is still working. My daddy used to rest his feet on the desk while I lay on the ground drawing.

"Come on, Melissa. Time to get ready for bed," Mama told me.

"But I'm not finished with my drawing!"

Mama gave me her sternest look, so I quickly shoved the unfinished drawing and colored pencils into the drawer that my parents allowed me to have as my own, then grumbled while I headed to the bathroom to brush my teeth. The picture would have to wait till the next day.

I blink back the memory, ignoring the dull ache in my head, and open the small drawer to my left. It must have belonged to me once upon a time, because inside are children's things: colored pencils, smiley face and sun shaped erasers, papers, and a notebook.

"*Oh,*" I breathe, peeking inside the drawer.

I pull out the notebook and stare at the cover. Lissy's Thoughts had been written on the top with an orange crayon. My journal? I flip through and see many childlike drawings, mostly trees and what looks like forts, with the occasional animal and . . . a unicorn? I can't tell. I guess I hadn't been much of an artist. I ignore the words written in the notebook. Though it's both tempting and scary to read what's inside, I set it on top of the desk for later. I want to take my time looking through it, so I'll finish looking through the desk for now.

I close the drawer and open the top middle drawer. Nothing exciting in there—writing utensils, a stapler, batteries, and a few other items one would find in a junk drawer. I look through the other drawers and find old checkbook registers, bank statements, some books that should be on a bookshelf and not in drawers, and other unimportant things.

I'm about to leave the desk after not finding anything great, when something in the bottom drawer catches my eye. It's an envelope, and some photos are sticking out of the top. There aren't many photos around the house except some of me alone or with my parents, but this stack shows many people. I look through them and see quite a few of me playing or swimming as a child—I had to be around four or five—and then more photos showing an older me, maybe six or eight. There are some with my parents and other adults at a picnic table or by the pool. I'm staring at the photos, wondering who everyone is. I don't think I have aunts or uncles. Maybe they're my parents' friends. And where are they all now?

I continue sifting through the pictures, and then, at the bottom of the stack, I find three photos of me . . . with a little boy. The boy is shorter than me and quite thin. He smiles big, making creases under his round, brown eyes. He looks so happy. In one photo, he has his arm around me, while I appear to be laughing at something, my eyes squinted as if blinded by the sun; another photo shows us during the winter in our snowsuits and boots, standing next to two snow people. The third photo is of us curled up on a pile of blankets next to a woodstove—my woodstove?—and we're reading books. We look so peaceful. Calm. Happy.

Could this be Jeff? Could this be the boy Megan mentioned? The boy I drew pictures of? What happened to him?

"Help!"

My heart pounds as I spring from the chair. That cry was not a product of my own mind; it came from outside. Racing into the kitchen, I peer through the window above the sink and catch sight of something dashing into the cornfield. Was it a person? Could it have been the one who had called out? It certainly hadn't been a child's voice—more like that of a man. Or had I merely imagined it all?

Driven by my insatiable curiosity, I quickly slip on a

sweater hanging by the door and dart outside. Stepping onto the sidewalk, I glance around, seeing nothing except for a few birds fluttering about. The wind begins to pick up, and the sky remains dark. Across the street, Sam's car is nowhere to be seen, unless he tucked it away in the garage.

"Help!"

That voice again! It's coming from the cornfield! Is there a kid who got lost in there?

Without giving it a second thought, I run to the cornfield and pause briefly before bolting through the stalks. They stand tall, a little over my head, and it's hard to see with the sky being dark. I'm not sure what direction I should be running in.

"Hello?" I call out. "Is someone there? Do you need help?"

I hear nothing and slow my steps, pushing through the pointy stalks, my feet kicking up dirt as I go. It's so difficult to move through here because the rows are so narrow.

This is foolish, I think. *Do I even know what I am chasing? Or who?*

I turn to retrace my steps back to the house when I hear something. A faint whisper.

"You. Let. Me. Die."

What? I look around frantically, wondering who could

have said it. My heart is nearly beating out of my chest at this point. The wind pick has picked up, so it could have been my ears playing tricks on me. I'm not even sure if there's anyone in here!

Everything seems to be closing in on me, and I feel disoriented. The corn stalks block my view from the house or the road. I turn my body in a circle, trying to get my bearings. Panic begins to set in, and my breathing is labored. I must take deep breathes to control this. Panic attacks are no joke.

When I feel myself calm a little, I take off running in what I believe to be the direction I think is home, only to have rain begin to pour down. As I navigate through the murky landscape, slipping and nearly falling on several occasions, I use the corn stalks to steady myself. Just when I think I am out of the cornfield, I trip on something, landing face down in the mud. For a moment, I lie there stunned, unable to move. When I lift my head, I see a pair of muddy sneakers.

A searing pain courses through my head, then everything goes dark.

CHAPTER 21

I OPEN MY eyes and blink several times, fighting the relentless rain and clearing away the fog from passing out. *How long was I out?* Then I remember the sneakers I saw. Someone had been standing here!

I slowly stand, still a little unsteady from my fall, and glance around. Just me and the cornstalks. I've got to get out of here! I quicken my steps to get the hell out of here and back to the house. The rain reduces visibility and makes the ground squishy underfoot, and it's a struggle to keep going. I finally burst through the edge of the cornfield and scream when someone grabs me.

"Melissa!"

It's Sam. I'm crying now as I fall into his arms, shaking

with fear. I can't help myself. He holds me, then silently leads me toward my house. When we get to the porch, I slip my sneakers off and walk inside the kitchen. It's warmer inside and being inside the house makes me feel more secure. Sam gently leads me to a chair where I sit.

"What happened?" he whispers.

I look up at him, tears drying on my face. I shake my head. "I heard . . . I thought I saw someone. Someone was in the cornfield. Taunting me. They . . ." I can't finish.

Sam is quiet for a second before saying, "Melissa, there's no one out there."

"But I heard someone call for help."

He shakes his head, his eyes showing pity. For me. I don't want him to pity me. I *want* him to believe me.

Sam walks to the refrigerator and grabs the wine bottle, then pours a little into a nearby glass. "Here," he says, handing me the "calming liquid" I most certainly need. "This will help."

I take the glass gratefully and take a sip, willing myself to calm down.

"I think it's too much for you here."

"What does that mean?"

"Lissy—er, *Melissa*—you seem . . . frantic often. Tense. Scared, even. Maybe you shouldn't be here alone."

I ignore the fact that he used my childhood nickname

again. Maybe it's a common nickname. "I'm fine. I just had a bad morning. I mean, who the heck would be trying to scare me?"

Sam shakes his head. "Maybe it's all in your—"

"Do *not* tell me it's in my head. I know what I've been seeing and hearing. Someone is messing with me!"

I take a sip of my wine, my nerves now shot. I don't need this. I don't need any of this. I need Sam to believe me. And I need all of this nonsense to stop.

"Ok, ok. I didn't mean to offend." He is quite for a second. "Do you often have episodes where you pass out? Head trauma, or something that causes that?"

"What an odd question," I mumble.

"No, no, I only meant . . . well, I'm just asking."

So strange. This man is strange.

"I'm calling the cops. I have to. They may not believe me, but—"

"No!" Sam practically shouts.

My eyes widen and I lean back in the chair.

He tries to recover, but I'm not buying it. Sam does not want me to call the cops. "Look, you're tired, or confused. Let's get a fire started. Get it cozy in here. I can take care of you."

"I don't have any wood." I don't go on to mention that

the chimney should be inspected, cleaned out.

Sam nods and stands. "Ok. Then maybe—"

"I think I need to be alone." I stand up as I cut him off. I'm about to say goodbye and head to the bathroom to change my clothes when a thought hits me. "Sam. What were you doing outside of the cornfield? It's like . . . It's like you knew I was in there."

"Oh." His eyes widen, and he shrugs. "I thought I heard yelling and wanted to make sure you were ok."

"So *you* heard yelling, but you indicated that *I* am going crazy because *I* heard someone."

He is silent. I wait. After some awkward moments of silence, he sighs.

"I heard *you* yelling, Melissa. I honestly don't think anyone is—or was—out there."

Fine. But it is curious how he always seems to be around just when I need someone. I nod and don't give it another thought because frankly I'm tired of it all. I think this house is making me crazy. And I can't go crazy.

"I'll leave you alone. Call me if you need anything," Sam says as he walks out the door.

I walk my weary self to the bathroom, taking my time to clean up and put on fresh clothes. Deciding I don't need any more wine, I set the glass down and grab a water bottle instead.

I'm ready to collapse, so I head to the living room and settle on the couch, grabbing my fleece blanket and curling up in a ball. It takes me a few minutes to realize that the room is warmer than the kitchen.

I look over to the woodstove. There's a fire in it. And wood is sitting next to it.

CHAPTER 22

I SIT UP in the darkness. Something woke me up. I wait a few seconds for my eyes to adjust. I can hear the rain pattering against the window, but that isn't what woke me; I'm sure of it.

I hear something tapping on my window that doesn't sound like rain, so I lean over to get a better look. I can barely see because of the rain, but when I stare long enough, I see someone standing in the back yard. I jump back in fright, trembling in fear. Surely, there is no one there and I imagined it.

There's that noise again. It sounds like something hitting the window, almost like a stone. *Is someone throwing stones at my window? Who? And why?*

"Psst! Lissy!"

I leaned my head out the window. "Stop throwing stones at my window. You're going to get me in trouble."

He simply grinned. "No one can hear. I wanted to wake you up."

I yawn and shake my head. "It's stupid o'clock in the morning. Go home and go back to bed."

"Let's go to our fort. I'm bored. I can't sleep."

He is whining now. I shake my head again and wave, then pull the window shut. When I lay my head back onto the pillow, I can hear the stone again. Silly boy. Hope he goes back to bed.

"Jeff?" I whisper to the empty room. *Is he haunting me?*

I bury myself under the covers. The tapping sound stops and I eventually fall back asleep. I really hope I start to remember more about Jeff and what happened to him. *To me.*

* * * * *

I'm so tired the next morning. Dreams, sounds, restless legs. It had me in a fitful sleep all night. I'm still wondering who stacked wood by the fireplace and started the fire. It must have been Sam. Why would he do that, though? Or did he? Did I do it? Maybe I'm losing my mind. Slipping back into that place . . .

No! I won't go back there. Ever.

I sleepily make my way downstairs after dressing and start making coffee. While the coffee is perking, I sit at the kitchen table with my head in my hands. I'm so tired. Part of me wants to crawl back into bed and sleep the day away. What I'm doing here is useless. I should give up trying to figure out what happened to me and try to just live. I feel like I'm no closer to finding answers and am only more confused. Maybe the memories don't want to surface. And, truth be told, I'm feeling a little scared. Strange things keep happening here, and since no one has actually seen another person lurking about, it must be all in my head. I can't let this overtake me. I want to be independent!

When the coffee is done perking, I pull the pot off the burner to sit for a few minutes, then I pull on a flannel shirt and step outside. The morning air is crisp but not cold, and I relish the peacefulness of the country. I walk over to the cornfield where, just yesterday, I fell. What actually happened? I'm beginning to feel frightened as of late with my memory loss and strange things happening. Am I conjuring things up in my head? Or is someone playing games with me?

And why does it seem like Sam is always around when I need to be "rescued" or soon after I've seen or heard odd things? I discreetly glance across the road, but I don't see him, and the curtains in the window are closed.

I slowly walk through the rows of corn as the sun peaks out from behind some clouds, warming my body. I'm not afraid this time. I feel calm, and I'm not chasing a ghost that doesn't exist. I stop and close my eyes, letting my mind take me back . . .

"What if we get lost out here? I think we've gone too far," he said in a worried tone.

He was always worried. A scaredy-cat, really. I turned and grabbed his hand, and with a big smile, I said, "Let's go on an adventure! Like . . . like Alice in Wonderland!!"

His eyes lit up at that, and off we went, giggling and pretending we were like Alice, chasing a white rabbit.

Farther and farther into the field we went . . .

I open my eyes and take a deep breath. I both love and hate the memories that have been invading my head. Ever since I returned, they're slowly seeping in. That's a good thing, right?

I walk back to the house and am pouring a mug of coffee when I hear the porch door open. I wait.

"Knock-knock!"

Megan.

I open the kitchen door and gesture for her to come in,

then pour her a mug of coffee. I'm becoming accustomed to acting as hostess around here. I don't mind at all; I welcome the company.

Megan graciously accepts the coffee, and we sit at the table.

"You look like hell."

"What does hell look like?" I sip my coffee, embracing the thought of being caffeinated.

Megan laughs. "Smartass."

"Megan, tell me about Jeff." I'm blunt, not even making small talk, just wanting to get to the point.

She is silent for longer than I like. Her eyes are downcast, and she finally sighs. "He was your best friend."

I set my mug down and put my head in my hands. "What happened to him?"

"You . . . Well, there was an accident. I don't know much."

I close my eyes and think. *Please, mind, think. Remember!* Nothing.

A cell phone rings, breaking me out of my trance. It's Megan's.

"Hey, Rach."

While Megan talks to her sister, I get up and grab some fruit from the fridge, set it on the table, then top my coffee off. She only talks for a few minutes, and I try not to listen in on the conversation.

"Rachel wants me to babysit tonight." Megan pops some fruit in her mouth, then downs her coffee. "I better get home so I can do some work. Thanks for coffee!"

"Wait, Megan!" *No, no, no! Don't leave yet!*

She turns to me before walking out the door. "Some things are best left . . . in the past."

I sit there after she leaves, now wanting more than ever to remember. Why does it seem I get so far only to be shut down by the people who know what happened? I'm so frustrated! I need to find out more about Jeff, not understanding why he must be kept a secret. I quickly eat and finish my coffee, and then am ready to finish weeding through the junk in the playroom.

After some time setting aside a few things and throwing away many things, I feel ready for a break. I'm happy at the progress I've made so far. The room was quite the disaster. I still can't fathom how it got that bad.

Before I take a break, I just want to clear off a smaller shelf full of games. I start tossing games into a large garbage bag—Smurfs . . . Monopoly . . . Hungry, Hungry Hippos—when a sharp pain stabs my head.

"I won! Woohoo!" he shouted, throwing the game piece across the

board.

I narrowed my eyes. "You cheated."

His eyes widen. "Did not!"

"Then let's rematch."

"Aww, Lissy, I'm bored. Let's go play in the barns."

"No, no, no! REMATCH!"

My eyes fly open, and the pain in my head is gone. These flashes of memories are annoying because they're bits and pieces. So frustrating!

Something hits the back door to the playroom, and I jump. It came from outside, which is where the door leads to. I stand quickly, nearly stumbling on my feet, and trip over boxes and bags while hurrying to the window. I catch a glimpse of someone running toward the barns. He or she is wearing jeans and a hooded sweatshirt with the hood pulled up, so I can't see who it is. I yank the door open and start running, yelling as I do.

"Hey! Stop! Who are you?"

I'm breathless and watch as the figure runs into the barns. I stop running because I need to be smarter. What would I actually do if I caught up with this person? Confront them? What if they're armed? No, this is not smart. I need to get back inside my house. Maybe I'll call 911 and the police can figure this out. I know what I saw.

They can at least find footprints.

I go through the back door and push it shut tightly and stand there.

Slam!

The front door. *The kitchen! Is someone in the house?* I pause, waiting to hear something else, while wondering why this person slammed the door. You'd think they'd want to be quiet to sneak up on me. Not this person. They *want* to be heard.

I hear footsteps. Slow. Deliberate. They're small though, almost like a child's. *What in the world?*

I hurry over to the couch and climb onto it, listening. The footsteps stop. They might come into this room! I hoist myself up onto the tall cabinet that stands in the doorway between the playroom and the hallway. From there, I lean over and hop over the railing to the staircase and run up. It was easier when I was a kid and could sneak through the two missing railing posts and onto the stairs instead of climbing over the rail.

At the top of the stairs, I hear a door creak open. The playroom! The intruder is looking in the playroom. I stand still, my heart hammering in my chest. The door closes and I hear the steps again. They're coming to the hallway door! I look around frantically. I can run through my bedroom and get to the kitchen the back way, grab something to use as a weapon, and wait for the intruder, but I'm scared half to death. They seem to be lurking slowly, but if they hear me coming through to the kitchen, they could run to catch up with me.

Of course, if the intruder is a child, I don't have to worry. But why would it be a child? Someone on a dare? Seems ridiculous, but I'm grasping at straws. I'm also not about to take chances. I look around, thinking.

The attic!

I grab the door handle and slowly turn it, willing it not to creak, and slip inside. I'm pulling the door closed when I hear footsteps start to come up the stairs. *Shit. Did they hear the door close? I don't think it made noise.*

I turn around and face the mounds of stuff piled in the attic, then scamper across, trying not to trip over anything. I could hide under any of these piles, and I am sure no one would find me unless they wanted to tear through everything. Instead, I opt to go into the crawlspace. I slide through, and, after closing the door, I crawl blindly through the darkness. Occasionally, I feel myself brush against something, but it must be the boxes I spotted when I first peeked in here the first time I looked through the attic. I'm praying I don't crawl through any cobwebs or come across a dead mouse or rat.

I finally come to a wall and can't go further, so I huddle there in the dark. I'm kicking myself for not having my phone on me. Rule number one of being in a house alone is always carry your phone with you. Just in case. And, apparently in my case, a weapon wouldn't hurt.

I close my eyes and practice my breathing. Deep breath in slowly, count to four; release breath slowly, count to four. Repeat. This was supposed to be easy—me, coming home to live. It was never meant to be about running away from people or things—ghosts of the past. I rock back and forth, suppressing the urge to scream or cry. I'm alone and very frightened.

Suddenly, I hear a noise. It sounds like someone came in; I can hear rustling of bags, so they must be walking through, not caring if they make noise. Maybe they'll trip over something and get hurt.

I wait a good five minutes before slowly crawling over to the door. Then I listen. Nothing. Where did the person go?

I am about to reach for the door handle when I feel something cold brush against my neck, and someone whispers, "*You. Left. Me. To. Die.*"

CHAPTER 23

I OPEN MY eyes to darkness. The air is stuffy and I am having trouble breathing. I struggle to pull in a deep breath, smelling only musty and stale air. *Where am I?* I put my arm out and feel a wall. No, a door! I'm in the attic crawl space! I must have passed out. *But why?*

I open the door and hurry out, looking around and not caring if someone is still here. I can't stay in this space!

There's no one here with me, though I didn't expect there to be. I practically run out of the attic, which is frustrating because there's so many things blocking my way, but I finally make it out the door. I don't bother closing it behind me. I just run. Down the stairs and through the living room and the kitchen. I make it outside, almost completely out of breath. I breathe in deep and then plop into the lawn chair. I don't realize I have tears running down my face until I taste salt. *Damnit!* I don't want to cry. I'm stronger than this.

I angrily wipe away my tears when I hear a twig snapping. I sit up and whip my head around. It's only Sam. Sam, who is always there when I need someone. Sam, whose providential appearances are unnerving. I sigh and sit back.

"Hey, are you ok? I was getting my mail and saw you run outside. You—you're crying."

Sam crouches down and looks at me with concern. I try to steady my breathing so I don't start bawling. I fear I am coming undone, so I sniffle and try to smile a little. I both like and despise this man. I still don't know who he really is, why he is here, and why he always seems to come to my rescue. But he *is* here now, and no one else is. Plus, if he wanted to kill me, he'd have done it by now.

"I'm ok. Just had a scare, that's all."

He doesn't say anything but pulls up another chair and sits near me. We don't say anything for a few minutes, and I notice the sun is high in the sky and it's quite warm. I wonder what time it is.

"I have an idea," Sam says suddenly. "Why don't you

let me spend a few nights here? You know, keep an eye on you and make sure you're safe."

I laugh; I can't help it. "Sam, I don't need a bodyguard. I'm fine, really." As if I would let him stay.

"You don't seem fine," he snaps. My eyes widen and he forces a smile. "Sorry. I'm sorry. I'm just concerned about you."

I sit back and close my eyes. The sun is warming my body enough to where I may need shorts today. The thought makes me smile. For a moment, I forget Sam is even sitting next to me.

"Sam," I say suddenly, remembering something. "A little while ago . . . er, this morning, I think, I saw someone wearing a hooded sweatshirt and they were running toward the barns."

"I haven't been out until now, but I glance out the window on occasion if I'm walking by." *Of course he does.* "Do you want me to look around? Check things out?"

I massage my temples, wishing this nightmare would end. Wishing Sam wasn't here or living across the road, but at the same time glad he's been around. How can I feel both safe and scared with him around?

Sam stands and looks around. Before I can tell him he doesn't have to look around, he starts walking toward the barns.

"I'll just take a look-see," he calls out.

I sigh and sit back, closing my eyes. Fine. Let him go. I need to rest for a minute, and I'd rather him investigate anyway. The breeze ruffles my hair a little, and the air smells slightly of fall, though it is quite warm. It isn't fall quite yet, but it will be here soon enough. Will I still be here? *Should* I still be here? I have no idea. I don't know what to do. I have nowhere else to go. My father kept this house for me to return to, but with everything strange happening, and me being scared out of my wits more often than not, maybe I should think of moving. I'd have to go back to the house where I lived for years, which is basically assisted living for people with . . . troubles. And I'm past that; I know I am! The only other option is finding a cheap apartment. Gee, I wouldn't even know where to begin finding one. It all sounds so tiring.

My eyes fly open at the sound of a pickup truck barreling down the road, and I stand up in disgust. Why do people have to drive so fast on these country roads? Gosh, they could kill an animal, or even a person!

Shaking my head, I stand and look around me. No sign of Sam. Where the hell is he? Well, he's a grown man; he can fend for himself. Instead of going to look for him, I head to the kitchen to grab some water, and after taking a few refreshing sips, my head feels clearer. I guess I should check out more of the house to keep my mind off of things that recently happened. It sounds better than sitting around and thinking.

I walk over to the "old part of the house" to check it out. The last time I was in that part was to walk through after I explored the attic. Now seems like a good time to look around, while Sam is checking out the barns.

I step onto the creaking wooden floor of the porch, and the faint scent of dust tickles my nose. The weather is still gloomy, and the sky is dark above, but I appreciate the musty smell of rain that hangs in the air. It doesn't take long for me to realize that the smell of rain is one of my favorite things.

There's a cluttered shelf lining the walls; its content is obscured by layers of dust and cobwebs. I pause at the sight of the blankets of cobwebs, layered and darkened by dust. Luckily, I don't see any spiders crawling around. I really need to get a broom one day and come out here and knock them all down. I wonder if there's someone I can hire to go through the house and porches to get rid of the cobwebs. I really do detest them.

I stare at the shelf before me, wondering why anyone would leave a shelf lying around outside like this? I notice a few books, and when I look closer, I see they are encyclopedias and a few volumes on chemistry. On another shelf are tiny carved animals, and I take a closer look. There's a horse and a cow . . . chickens. A flash image of me running through the barn as a kid, just past my dad as he milks the cow, comes to mind, and I suck in a breath. I step away from the carved animals and give the shelf a once-over. Yeah, I'll be throwing this out too, except for the books and those carved animals.

As I reach the end of the porch, my eyes fall on a trunk nestled in the corner, its lid slightly ajar. It's wooden with a flowery pattern carved on it. I kneel and reach for it with a hesitant hand (who doesn't love a good look-see into an old trunk?) and push it open, the hinges groaning in protest. Inside is a jumble of toys and books. I spot a tiny woolen sock. Everything looks dusty and dirty, and even though I worry about spiders, I dig in, sifting through the contents of the battered trunk. My fingers brush against something small and fragile nestled near the bottom. I tug at it until I pull free a small, faded baby-blue blanket.

My breath catches in my throat as I gingerly lift the blanket up to look at it better. Just then, a wave hits me as a splitting headache takes over.

When I open my eyes, I'm lying down on the ground, just beside the trunk. I must have fallen. The baby-blue blanket is still in my hands, and the residue of the last headache I had is still strumming a faint beat. This time there had been no memory, just a blackout. These blackouts have been coming more consistently, and I'm not sure if it's a good or bad thing. Hey, I mean, my memory is being put to work, right? That's what I've always wanted—to recover my memories.

Pushing myself up, I set the blanket aside. This probably belongs to someone else. I think it's very creepy that it's here, though. All this weird stuff in the house that doesn't seem like it belongs. How long has this house been abandoned for? Maybe someone dumped this trunk here and left; it does look battered down and weathered. It couldn't belong to my parents. I don't think.

I stare at the trunk for a bit, then start to rummage through it once more. Maybe I'll find something else that can help me. I feel tears well up in my eyes. I wish my parents were here to hold me, talk to me, tell me what the hell happened and what is going on now. Even my grandma can't help me now. I'm alone. It doesn't matter if Sam is across the road or Megan and Rachel are up the road; when it all comes down to it, I am alone.

I take a few deep breaths just like I learned in therapy and push on. There's more junk in the trunk, and after I eventually bring everything out, there's nothing interesting to find anymore. *Great.* I'll probably throw this trunk in the trash with the rest of the things in it.

I set to work, rearranging everything I pulled out of the trunk before sliding it back against the wall. The lid creaks close.

My growling stomach tells me it's past lunch time. I can't believe how long I've been rifling through junk! *What time* is *it?*

Then I remember something . . .

Sam!

Had he come up from looking in the barns and went home? Why wouldn't he tell me he was going home? Unless he couldn't find me. That must be it.

I walk away from the porch, then make a detour toward the barn. "Sam!" I yell out. Nothing. I take two more steps toward the barn. "Sam, are you there?" Nothing. I back away from the barns and head back into the house. I'm not going into any of those barns unarmed. Sam probably left. Or not.

I wipe my hands on my jeans as I walk on to the house, looking over at Sam's house. There's no one around; all is silent. Not even a dog barking. It must be late afternoon because the sun is lowering. *Crap. I wasted an entire day!*

I head to the other porch and go through and into the

kitchen. There's plenty of light coming through the windows, so I don't bother turning the light on.

After washing my hands, I make myself a peanut butter and jelly sandwich and pull out a bag of potato chips from the cupboard. I eat quickly, wanting to check the barns to see if Sam is still down there. I'm still worried that I didn't hear from him. What if he fell through a loose board and is hurt? Maybe I should bring my bat in case there is someone down there. Maybe they hurt Sam!

It's getting chilly out, so I throw on a sweater and head down the driveway to the main barn. It looks dark. Ominous. I shudder and walk through the entrance.

"Hello? Sam?" I call. My voice echoes along the vast space. I look around but only see what's been there since I've returned: bales of hay stacked around the room, a large machine of some sort, rusted from what I can see. That's it.

I walk around not really expecting to see Sam but wanting to look in case he is hurt somewhere. Then again, he'd yell . . . I think. Maybe I wouldn't hear him, though.

I walk out, ready to head into the next barn, when I hear something. My head swivels around, and I realize the sound is coming from the silo. Faint sounds of children talking and laughing fill my ears, but I know it's all in my head. My heart begins to race. I don't like the silo. I'm not allowed near it. I'm not allowed in it.

I step forward, stumbling over my feet, now shaking with fear. Memories start picking at my mind like an ice pick.

He fell . . . fell . . . fell . . .

Sam's voice comes back in my head. *"Maybe he didn't hang on long enough."*

"Melissa! Help me!"

That's a man's voice! Sam?

I start running up to the house. I have no idea why I'm terrified, or why someone is calling out to me clear as day from the silo, but I know something's not right. *What happened in that silo? Who fell? And who is calling me now?*

I don't notice the tears that slip out of my eyes until I make it to my house and bend over, hurting from being so out of breath. When I'm finally able to breathe normally, I look behind me. The sun is almost completely set now, and darkness is setting in. The barns and silos look more foreboding than ever.

Where the hell is Sam?

I stand there for a moment, somehow managing to keep my composure. I was half expecting to be chased down by the figure that lived in the barns. *Did they get Sam?*

And the silo. The terror I'd felt had begun immediately when I heard the voice coming from the silo. I decide to walk across the road and look for him. Taking more deep breaths to calm down, I head toward Sam's house, but as I'm halfway there, something prompts me to turn around.

I see a light coming from the kitchen window. I never turned the light on this morning because the sun was coming through the windows, and even when I grabbed a sandwich, it was light enough to see without using electricity. But it's on now.

The light suddenly goes off. Then it flickers on again.

CHAPTER 24

THROUGHOUT MY LIFE, I've had plenty of time to read books, my favorites being murder mysteries and thrillers. My home was safe; I felt I could read whatever I wanted and never have to worry about anything bad happening to me. But now I'm alone. In the country. With a strange neighbor I barely know. Maybe I should switch to reading sappy romance novels.

I abandon the thought of going to look for Sam and run back to my house and over to the old part of the house, then go inside to find something I can use as a weapon if needed. After a bit of searching, I find a crowbar. Perfect. I considered using my trusty bat, but a crowbar seems like a better weapon. It's heavy, but I can yield it if I need to.

Carrying the crowbar, I walk across the lawn and step onto the front porch. I don't hear anything, but I'm not exactly expecting to.

I enter the kitchen. It's empty. I mean, no one is here. I set the crowbar down and think for a minute. *Who could have turned the lights on? Sam?* I can search the house, but honestly, I'm tired and over all of this. I sit at the kitchen table for a few minutes, thinking things over. For years, nothing strange happened, and now that I'm in my childhood home, tons of strange things are happening. Maybe my therapists were right; maybe I'm not cut out to be on my own. But if that were the case, they'd never have allowed me to leave.

I want to give up and leave, but I know I can't. Not now anyway. The logical part of me says to search the house and spend my days cleaning everything out and getting organized. Then I can decide if I want to stay or leave.

I pick the crowbar up and hurry from room to room so any intruder won't have a chance to leave before I notice, turning lights on as I go and intending to leave them on.

Laundry room—empty.

Living room—empty.

Playroom—empty.

Hallway—empty.

Every room upstairs—empty.

By the time I get back downstairs to the kitchen, I'm

laughing at myself. Out loud. How ridiculous to think someone is hiding in my house. And it's certainly not haunted. There's probably something wrong with the lights. My mind was just saying negative and scary things to me just like it used to, wanting me to give up. But I won't.

I set the crowbar next to the door and wash my hands before putting a Hot Pocket in the microwave. I've never had one of these, but the grocery store sells them and I love ham and cheese, so I figured, why not!

While the Hot Pocket is cooking in the microwave, I pour myself a glass of wine and take a sip. A Hot Pocket and glass of wine for dinner. How very redneck. I giggle a little. I think being at this house has turned me into a wine-loving fool.

The microwave beeps, signaling my dinner is done, so I pull it out and cut it up. Steam comes out of the gooey ham and cheesy goodness and I take a bite, not caring that my mouth is now burned.

After I finish eating, and draining the wine that's in my glass, I look around. Now what? I'll have to check on Sam in the morning, and if I can't find him, I'll call for help. Maybe Megan can help me out. I really am not terribly worried, as Sam is a grown man. Something, however, niggles at my mind. I push it away. I'm not heartless; just helpless in this situation.

A thump from upstairs tells me that's the next thing I should be worrying about and where I need to go. The sound came from above, which means that extra bedroom I found but hadn't looked through yet. It's dark out now, but I am wide awake and ready to tackle whatever is inside. Even if it means someone is in there, waiting to attack me. But if they were going to attack, they'd have done it by now. I think someone is merely trying to spook me. Or make me lose my mind. Well, it gets to the point where you're tired of being spooked and scared and just want to be done with the bullshit. I guess I have reached that point now.

After grabbing a flashlight and the crowbar, I head up the steep wooden steps and into the bedroom. I flip the switch to a nearby lamp and look around. The room smells musty and old, something I hadn't noticed the first time I peeked inside. To my right is a door, which I assume leads to a closet. I didn't want to look in there when I first discovered this room, but now I feel I should.

I pull the door open and turn the flashlight on. Some empty hangars are on the rods but no clothes. On the floor of the closet are . . . toys. Stuffed animals and a variety of kids' toys. Strange. They must have been mine. There are quite a lot of toys just laying around in this house. Sam's book could come to a finish if he just explored here for a day.

I close the door and walk over the boxes sitting against the wall by the window. I open one and see clothes. But they're not girls' clothes. They're boys' clothes. *Why would my parents have a box of boys' clothes here?* I open another box. More clothes. Another reveals several pairs of boys' shoes. *What the hell?*

I open the last box. Books and notebooks. I pull a notebook out and flip through. It appears to be a school notebook, but there's no name. I assume they're all mine.

I pick up another notebook, and this one has drawings. Many are of animals, it seems, but there are a few pages with two kids, a girl and a boy, holding hands and smiling. The girl has brown hair, as does the boy. They look alike. I squint to read what is written under one of the pictures and gasp. I throw the notebook into the box and scramble to my feet, swaying in the process, just as another memory hits me.

We were all happy; Mommy, Daddy, and even me.

"Mommy, is it a boy or a girl?"

Mommy laughed and Daddy said, "He's a boy."

"Can I hold him?"

"Well, yes, you can, honey, but only if you're sitting and one of us

is with you. He's very small and fragile still."

I looked down into the baby cot at the tiny person. He was so small.

"He looks like maconi!"

Mommy and Daddy burst out laughing at that and I giggled. "He does look like a little macaroni, doesn't he?" Daddy said.

"He's Mac," I said, clearly enjoying my moment.

"I'm really going to call him that," Daddy said to Mommy, who swatted his arm playfully.

Memories, long buried beneath the layers of my subconscious, start to stir—a soft cry in the night, the gentle touch of a tiny hand . . . his eyes as they flutter open and then focus on me.

"No. No, no, no." I shake my head and back out of the room. Time to get another glass of wine. Maybe the bottle.

I run down the stairs and into the kitchen as if my life depends on it.

*****

"Come on, Melissa, our lunch is going to get spoiled."

I hated it when he whined. We were the same age, but he often acted like such a baby. But Mama always told me to take a deep breath and let it out slowly when I felt frustrated. So that's what I did. I drew the line at counting to ten. No one has time for that.

"Ok," I said slowly after releasing my breath. "Just one more

thing."

I carefully tucked my doll in with the dark blue blanket, gave her a pat on the head, and stood up.

"I'm ready now. Happy?"

He merely stuck his tongue out at me. I smacked his arm and ran ahead. "You're it!" I shouted, running down the stairs, through the kitchen, and into the front yard. He ran after me, laughing and panting from being out of breath.

When we stopped by the tree swing, he said, "Lissy, why is that doll so special? And why does she sleep in—"

"Shh!" I whispered fiercely, looking around to make sure no adult was near. "We're not allowed in that room. Mama doesn't know."

"Then why—"

"Because Kristi is special to me and she needs to sleep in that room. You wouldn't understand."

He didn't say anything for a moment, then he reached for my hand. I let him take it because that was his way. He was very sensitive and knew when I was sad.

"Ok," he said.

We stood by the swing for a few seconds until I heard his mom yell from across the road. Time for him to go home.

CHAPTER 25

I DOWN TWO more glasses of wine and walk outside into the cool night air, swaying slightly. At least my nerves are settled. Maybe I will just be a hermit and drink wine all the time. Who cares? I'm so discouraged. No one told me adulting was easy. Or maybe it would be if I wasn't living in a maybe-haunted house with a stalker who wants me to lose my mind.

It's so quiet up here in the country. I look around, seeing only shadows of the trees. Some stars dot the sky, but the moon is behind heavy clouds. I shiver a little. For a second, I forget that Sam went missing and I've done nothing today but get the wits scared out of me.

A glance across the road shows no lights on at Sam's

house. How can that be? He can't still be in the barns. I never heard anyone calling for help. I haven't seen him, either. Maybe he drove into town. But why didn't he check in with me to tell me what he found? If anything? Ugh, maybe I should have looked more thoroughly. After all, if he's hurt, it is on my land. I don't want to get sued.

This house and the barns spook me very badly, and all I want to do is leave. There seem to be many secrets from the past, but so far nothing has led me to find out why I was taken from my home as a child. I should probably stop trying to find answers and let it all go. It's not like it has an effect on me at this point. I'm an adult living on my own. It seems like the truth doesn't want to show itself to me, and I'm tired of searching for it. I'm also pretty stubborn and very curious.

A flashing light across the road pulls me out of my thoughts. I squint in the darkness. There it is again! It's a faint light past the window of Sam's house. *Is he there?* Maybe his power went out and he has a flashlight. *Or maybe he doesn't want to be seen*, a voice whispers in my mind.

I decide to ignore that voice and head across the road. It's stupid, I know, going into a house of a man I'm somewhat wary of and find out what a little flash of light is. Maybe I just don't care anymore.

I'm wearing only jeans and a sweatshirt, and it's quite cool out, but I press on, determined to find Sam—or whatever is in there.

I look both ways before crossing the road, which is silly considering it's nighttime and everything is dark. Clearly, no cars are approaching. Old habits, I guess.

"Jeff! You have to look and listen before crossing!" I scolded him because he was always trying to dart across the road without looking.

"Come on, I don't hear any cars. Let's just go."

He was whining again. I shook my head, thinking, One of these days, he's going to get himself killed.

He ran across the road, with me following.

I reel back, rooted in the middle of the road as that memory hits my mind. I squeeze my eyes shut for a moment, trying to remember more—a face, something!—but nothing comes. A distant howl pulls me out of my trance and my eyes open, looking again at Sam's house. I press on.

I head up the driveway slowly, keeping my eyes on the window in case I see the light again. When I reach the house, I decide to try the side door to the garage instead of the front door to the house. I check the handle. Unlocked. The door creaks open, and I peer inside the cold garage.

Sam's car is here. There's nothing else in the garage except a tall toolbox.

I go to the door that leads inside the house. To my left are the steps leading down to what I assume is the basement. No thank you. I will definitely not be checking that out. *But what if Sam is down there? And maybe he is hurt?* I shake my head to rid it of those thoughts. I will not check out the basement if I don't have to.

I walk up the three steps and look into the window of the door. I see a dim light coming from the kitchen area, which is probably from the clock on the stove. Everything else is dark.

I check the handle. Unlocked. For a second, I wonder if I'm really being smart about this. Of course I'm not. I'm going in anyway. I slowly open the door and quietly call out.

"Sam? Are you here?"

Silence.

I step into the kitchen and close the door behind me. *Now what?* I'm mentally kicking myself for not bringing the crowbar from my house. A glance to the right shows me there's a butcher block, so I grab the largest knife, hoping I don't have to use it. I feel safer with it in my hand, though.

I creep farther into the house, glancing around as I do. The house is empty and eerie. No sign of Sam. Or anyone.

I creep through the dining area and into the living room, where Sam and I sat having tea one evening. I then notice the sliding glass door is slightly open. *What in the world?* I creep toward it and peer in. There are shadows over everything, and I can't see very well without the light. I squint my eyes to get a better look but don't see anything different since the last time I looked in here.

I back out of the room and hurry back to the kitchen, determined to find a flashlight. Obviously, Sam is not here, so I don't mind snooping. *Unless he's in the basement hurt or dead.* I shake that thought off. No basement! I fish a flashlight from one of the kitchen drawers and step cautiously into the hallway of the house. My heart is pounding in my chest because I know I shouldn't be here, sneaking through Sam's home, trespassing. Yet, here I am. In my defense, I'm looking for him, so is it really trespassing?

The air suddenly feels very heavy, and I grip the flashlight tightly in my hand, making sure to take deep breaths. The light beam cuts through the darkness like a knife, and it spooks me to see how the thick darkness quickly returns as soon as the light beam shifts. Anything could jump at me from the dark, and I wouldn't see it coming.

Yeah, sure, the best way to go about this is by scaring yourself.

I want to go back to the sliding doors, but I ignore them for a minute. Curiosity could be the death of me, I tell you, but I can't stop myself from wanting to know what secrets lie about in this house. Every house has secrets, right? Also, there's a sense of familiarity here, and not because I was here drinking tea with Sam some days ago. I feel like I've been here before, long ago.

I will my mind to stir up memories—anything! Nothing pops up.

As I move deeper into the house, shadows dance and flicker across the walls, and I swear I'm seeing shapes that seem to shift and twist with every step I take. This is a sign to go back.

"Sam?" I call out in a weak voice. I'm not sure if I want to find him or not. If he was fine, he'd have shown himself to me by now.

I wait. Nothing. He's not home; I've already established that. But for some reason, I feel the need to justify why I'm here. I'm simply looking for a friend who disappeared. Yeah. I'm genuinely concerned; no ulterior motives here. I almost laugh at my guilty thoughts.

"Sam!" My voice echoes and hangs in the hollow, empty silence, unanswered.

My mind brings forth the sound of faint laughter. I

pause. I'd love to peek in the bedrooms, but more than likely, they're empty. Plus, what if Sam returns to find me rummaging through his stuff? I shake my head. Whirling back, I retrace my steps and actually want to head back home, but I spot the sliding glass doors I saw before, on the day I came here with Sam, and it's like a force, drawing me in. I've nearly forgotten that the reason I came here tonight in the first place was because I saw a light flicker. Or did I imagine it? Well, I'm here now. No going back.

"Just do it," I whisper to myself and walk toward the door. Everything in me is telling me to turn around with every step I take, yet I find myself in front of the forbidden doors. I gently pull, and the door slides with a squeak that resounds through the house. I stand still, listening. When I'm sure that no one is coming, I step into the room, and it's bathed in shadows, illuminated only by the glow of my flashlight. The air is stale and musty, like how a carpet would smell when someone spills water on it. The thick scent of neglect and decay wafts up toward me, and I clear my throat.

Quickly, I scan the room, taking in the sights. Boxes sit around the room, and there are forgotten toys strewn across the floor—a jumble of stuffed animals, action figures, and colorful building blocks. *Why does this look like the playroom in my house?* I train the flashlight on the walls, noting that a part of it is peeling off and that there's a rocking chair in a corner, just beside a shelf.

I've seen a number of shelves in my forgotten home, but the sight of *this* dusty shelf lined with children's books gives me a pause, and a chill suddenly blazes down my spine. I've seen this shelf before!

My hands tremble as I move closer to the wooden shelf. I reach out to touch the faded spines of the books, tucked tightly in their carriers. I can feel the memories stirring deep within my subconscious mind, and with it, the familiar heaviness that wraps itself around my head whenever I'm about to be racked by headaches.

"Come on," I whisper to myself. Well, to my brain *and* the shelf. "Tell me what you're hiding from me."

Dust twirls up from where my fingers have disturbed it on the shelf and tickles my nose. Trying not to sneeze, I look away, but that's when I see something. Something really familiar—a small wooden toy, its paint chipped and worn with age.

Suddenly, a bright flash of memory overtakes my mind, and I stumble backwards at the sheer force of it, landing on my bottom. I grab my head with both hands, eyes shut, feeling like I might erupt into a scream from the pain.

We were holding hands—Jeff and me. He said that's what best friends do, but I thought he just didn't want me to run off and leave him again. The sun was hot, and we were in a backyard. I was sweating from the heat, and his hands were slimy in mine.

"You have baby hands!"

"No, I don't!" He pulled his hand away, and I laughed, looking at him. His face was a shadow of crisscross lines, like how a channel with nothing but static would look, but I knew he wasn't happy. I called his hands baby hands.

"Baby hands, baby hands," I sang, and he started to walk away. He didn't like it when I teased him.

"Where are you going?"

"Home!"

"Come on!"

"No! Leave me alone."

"Sorry. Jeff!" I whined, but he kept going, and I helplessly watched him go, until suddenly he stopped, as if he saw something. Jeff bent down and took it from the ground, then he turned toward me.

"Look, Lissy! I found this toy in the bushes. It's like a treasure!" He waved it above his head at me.

"Oooh!" I ran to him.

"Come on, let's play King of the World with it!"

I loved King of the World because Jeff was king and I was the queen. It was a fun and silly game we made up. We did that a lot—make up games that none of the other kids were privy to. It was like having a secret club.

I groan and stare up at the shelf before me. This definitely used to be Jeff's home. I sit up because no intruder should be on the floor, leaning against the wall on the floor like that, just waiting to be caught. The flashlight is still in my hand.

As I struggle to stand, the flashlight beam wildly sweeps across the room, catching on to something lurking in the shadows—a glint of metal, half-hidden beneath a pile of discarded toys. I didn't notice it when I stood before the shelf.

Maybe it's another toy. I walk over and reach out to retrieve the object. It's very cold.

I bring it under the light, and my breath catches in my throat—a bloody knife! The blood is sticky on the metal, but some of it is still fresh.

"Oh my God!" I throw it down and start to run toward the door when a sudden noise startles me to a stop—a whisper coming from behind me in the shadows. I hear it as clear as day.

"Melissa."

It sounded like a little boy just said my name! Like how Jeff sounds in my memories.

No, no, no, it's all in my head. It's all in my head. At least I'm starting to remember him with every memory trigger I get. That's the good part, but I just saw a knife with fresh blood in Sam's house!

Pulling the slide door open, I flee the room, suppressing the panic that now courses through my body, on an adrenaline high. Forget Sam and any person who may be lurking in the shadows. I have to get out of here, fast!

Thoughts tumble through my head as I hurry through the house. Jeff had been my best friend. This was his house. His family left. Suddenly. That much is obvious, given that his toys are still here. *Why the hell was Sam crouched in here crying the night Megan and I found him?*

Why the hell does he have a bloody knife?! I start to wonder whose blood it is. Sam was crouched in a corner that day, and Megan and I saw him. Maybe he'd cut himself. No, that doesn't seem right; a grown man wouldn't be hunched over like that, crying over a cut hand.

I almost laugh in relief as I make it to the kitchen door. Turning for one final look, I glance over at the dining room table and see papers strewn all over. Sam's work. Panic aside, and not thinking that someone could be waiting to hurt me, I decide to take a look. *Of course* I'm going to take a look. I'm dying to know what Sam is writing about. If anything, it might tell me a little bit more about him. The man's been nothing but mystery.

I shine the flashlight over the pages. Some are handwritten, but most are typed. I pick one up and read.

She doesn't know what she's getting into. Stupid woman. How could she not see it coming? How could she not know? Her loss is his gain. He has his victim. She can't get away now. She will pay for what she did.

I drop the page like it's a hot potato. What the hell? I thought he said he was writing about the paranormal.

Suddenly, something makes me look to my left, where the picture window is. Someone is standing on the sidewalk in front of my porch!

CHAPTER 26

I GRIP THE butcher knife tighter in my hand and hurry out of the house, through the garage, and out the door. It's not until I'm in the driveway, heading down, that I realize how stupid and careless I'm being. I just spotted someone standing in front of my house, and I'm barreling over there like I'm going to overcome whatever awaits me. How stupid! Just like in the movies. No one thinks.

I stop in the middle of the driveway and stare across the road. No one is standing there.

What the hell? I saw someone. I know I did!

I glance back and don't see anyone, then press forward toward my house. *Get home; get inside; get safe*—that is all I can think of at this point.

Half walking, half running, I approach my porch, my heart still racing from everything! This entire place is scary as hell, and it's like I'm only now noticing that. I mean, I've been creeped out many times before since I came here, but it feels like I'm only now *feeling* the fear. I hesitate for a moment before cautiously stepping onto the front stoop. *What if the shadow I saw is a person and they're in my house right now, waiting for me on the other side of the door?* The panic I've been suppressing threatens to spill over any moment now.

I move to the side and crouch down to catch my breath and think. I can try to sneak inside—at least I have a knife and know how to use it if I need to—or I can walk up the road and bang on Rachel's door and get help. That second option doesn't appeal because there's no way I can walk up that road alone . . . in the dark . . . in the country. And despite how scared I am, I don't want to wake her kids and cause unnecessary turmoil. What about Megan? She'd help me! No. I must go inside my own house and face whatever is there—whatever fate awaits me.

The evening air is heavy with the smell of rain, the silence broken only by the distant chirping of crickets and my raggedy breathing. It's all too much! My nerves are scrambling; everything seems just so . . . creepy! And dangerous. Thankfully, the panic only lasts for a minute or so, and I just stand there in front of my house. Waiting in the darkness.

They were right. They were all right. I should've listened and moved on with my life anywhere but here. Coming back was wrong. But now that I am back, and I know something terrible happened when I was a child, I need to remember; I'm desperate to remember. *What happened to Jeff? Where* is *Jeff? Is someone in my house? In the barns? Am I crazy? Is that why we had to leave? My mother, in her diary, said I was a crazy person, and maybe she was right!*

Where the hell is Sam? If he's not home and his car's there, did he ever leave the barn? I tell myself he is a grown man and I am not going to worry about it, but my mind won't stop reeling with thoughts.

The thoughts and questions continue to jostle in my head, but I shake them off and make the decision to go in. I might as well face my fear. A howl breaks silence, and I nervously look up from the door to scan the area. It didn't sound close by, but still. I am beyond paranoid at this point.

I push the door open, stumbling through and expecting to find someone on the other side. There's no one. Slamming the door shut behind me, my breath comes in ragged gasps as I lean against it. For a moment, I stand there in the dimly lit kitchen, listening for any sign of intruders or any hint of danger lurking just beyond the threshold. But all

I hear is the quiet hum of the refrigerator and the distant ticking of the clock on the wall.

I decide I need to call the police again. This time they will take me seriously—the knife, the papers of the story from Sam! They *must* take me seriously!

I make sure I turn on as many lights as I can to feel safer, then call the police. After what seems like forever, I hear a car door slam, then I run outside. I come to a halt when I see Giganto climb out of the car. No one else is with him. Damnit. Not him. And why did he come out here alone? He slams the door shut and stands there, staring at me. I stare back. It's a face-off. Finally, he steps forward and begins to walk toward me.

"Ms. Turner," he mutters, no emotion in his voice.

"Melissa," I snap. "Thanks for finally getting here."

"What is it this time, Melissa?"

Oh, I do not like this policeman. Instead of snapping at him, I tell him everything that has happened: Sam going missing, the knife, the papers, all of it. He listens, jotting something down in his notebook on occasion, but mostly looking bored or raising his eyebrows.

When I finish, I shift awkwardly on my feet, waiting. Will he say it's all in my head? They always do. Maybe he'll surprise me and check things out. I have no idea what to expect and no clue why he came alone. Don't police show up in twos?

To my surprise, he says, "Ok, I'll check things out. Why don't you wait inside?" He nods toward the house, and I find myself happily agreeing. He has a gun; I do not. He can look around all he wants. I'll be safe inside. Or not.

I pace the kitchen for the next twenty minutes, and finally there's a slight knock on my door. I pull it open and gesture for Giganto to come in. He has a serious look on his face.

"Well, what did you find?" I demand. He can't think I'm crazy now. There's evidence!

"Ms. Turner—er, Melissa," he starts, rubbing a hand over his jaw, looking carefully at me. "I searched the house across the road. There was nothing alarming there. In fact, it doesn't even look like anyone lives there but for some boxes. Maybe someone was passing through and used the house to stay. You know, we do get the occasional squatter around here."

The what*? No. No, that can't be right. I've been there. I've been to Sam's house! I've seen him. Talked to him! Went to breakfast with him. Wait . . .*

"Breakfast! We went to town recently and had breakfast together. Call them. Surely someone remembers us. Oh, and there was a couple who came to speak to us. And then

Sam didn't even eat his pancakes, just left them there."

Oh. Shouldn't have said that. But I know we went to breakfast together; we even road in Sam's car. How could I make that up?

Giganto sighs. "Look, we've been up here, looked through the barns, the house, the property. Tonight I checked out the house across the road. Nothing. No one."

"No." I shake my head and start to pace. "No, that's not right. There *is* someone. Sam. His name is Sam. He's a writer. I've been over there. He has pages of his book on the table, and the back room is full of toys and stuff. I saw it!"

The officer has the audacity to look concerned. Concerned! He doesn't believe me; I know that.

"Melissa, there were no pages, no knife, no . . . toys. Just some boxes. Doesn't look like anyone lives there. Are you sure that you—"

"That I what?" I spit out. "I'm sure of everything I saw. Someone is messing with me. It must be Sam. He's gone missing. He's behind this!" I feel out of control at this point. I'm looking around wildly, almost like I'm expecting Sam or some sort of clue to pop up. Officer Monroe doesn't believe me.

"What about the bedrooms?" I ask suddenly. "Sam lives

there. He must sleep in one of the bedrooms."

"The beds in the three bedrooms were made up, but didn't appear that anyone slept in them, and there are no clothes in the dressers. Nothing in the bathroom that would indicate someone is occupying the house."

I want to scream in frustration. Sam lives there. I know it! Where else would he shower and change his clothes? I've got to convince the officer that Sam has been living there.

Wait. Megan!

I look up with hope. "Megan. Up the road! She saw Sam. She knows he lives there. She'll vouch for me!"

The officer looks skeptical, but he takes down the information anyway. We talk for a few more minutes, and he turns to leave. I can't believe he's going. Nothing has been resolved. I feel so helpless.

After Officer Giganto leaves, I storm into the living room and plop onto the couch, angry but unable to shake the feeling of unease that still lingers. The memory of the figure standing outside my house haunts my thoughts, with Sam's disappearance as an added weight. A gnawing feeling of fear starts to overcome me. I feel tears pool in my eyes, threatening to roll down my face. *Why, why, why?* I left my so-called "home" to come back to my true home and carry on with life. Sure, finding out what happened in the past was definitely on my radar, but to be tortured was certainly not. And that's what is happening. Someone is torturing me.

I can't sit here. I need to pace. Or do something! I sit up and wipe the tears from my eyes and take a deep breath. Before I stand, I hear a door creak. It's coming from upstairs! I jump up off the couch and go to the door that leads to the stairway. No way am I opening the door just yet, so I put my head against the door, willing my ear to hear something. Nothing. I turn the door handle slowly—of course it squeaks as it always has—and reach my hand out to flip the light switch on. I look up but don't see anyone. What does startle me is seeing the attic door open. I had closed that and locked it the last time I was upstairs. Is someone in there?

Whether an adrenaline rush from fear or just plain stupidity, I find myself running up the stairs two at a time and swinging the attic door open fully. The stale air hits my face, and I grimace but take a deep breath and step through the threshold. I don't have a flashlight, and it's very dark but for the hall light behind me. I leave the door open and slowly creep through the large room, looking left and right but keeping my ears open for any hint of sound—of movement.

Suddenly, the door behind me slams shut and I hear a click. I run to the door, stumbling over piles of junk and nearly falling on my face as I do, but when I reach the door, I find it locked. I start banging on it, screaming for whoever is out there to let me out. It's not a ghost; there's someone in my house! I pound on the door but soon realize that's just taking up energy I don't want to sap out right now. Instead of taking my anger out on the door, I turn and climb over all the crap in this damn attic until I get to the door in the floor. The one that leads downstairs. I pull the door up and stumble blindly in the dark, with only the wall as support, and finally make it to the bottom of the stairs without breaking my neck. I reach for the door handle.

Locked.

I'm trapped.

CHAPTER 27

WHERE AM I?

I sit up and groan, opening my eyes to see darkness. I jump to my feet and feel around, my head spinning as I do. I realize I'm at the bottom of the stairs still, in front of the door to the old part of the house. *How long have I been out? Did I pass out? What is going on with me??*

I stand there for a moment, trying to wrap my head around everything—getting locked in the attic and its stairwell for God knows how long, passing out—but then I take a few deep breaths in an out like my therapist taught me and reach for the door handle. I don't expect it to turn, but when it does, I am shocked. I stumble through the door into the old part of the house and glance wildly around me, checking for any intruder. But I can't see anything. It's dark.

I slowly make my way toward the door that leads to the porch and step out, breathing in the night air. There is no rain, just a slight breeze, and I cannot hear a thing. It's like the world is silent around me. It's almost eerie. I walk slowly across the front lawn to the other side of the house—the main entrance that I always use—turning my head to look at Sam's house as I walk. It's dark. *Where is that man? It's like he just . . . vanished!*

I'm shaking as I walk to the other porch to head inside. Wait. Whoever locked me in . . . Won't they be inside, waiting? No. I have to go in. I need water, and I'm definitely not staying out here. I keep thinking if they want to kill me, they would have already.

I make haste to the front door and walk bravely into the kitchen. There's no murderer or squatter sitting at the table. I hurry to the fridge to gulp down some water before pouring a generous glass of wine. I almost grab something to snack on, but I'm so on edge, I'm not even hungry.

I kick my sneakers off at the front door and realize I have to pee really badly, so I quickly relieve myself, switch from jeans to pajama bottoms, and take my glass into the living room. I nearly drop the glass when I walk in. There's a soft glow and it's coming from the woodstove. Someone started a fire in here! Now I'm convinced there's an intruder—maybe a squatter? I've heard of them being in this area—and I give a resigned sigh. Nothing I can do now. It's nighttime; it's dark. I'm tired and sore from crouching in that damn stairwell. So instead of searching for a squatter or possible murderer, I curl up on the couch with my wine and let thoughts of the day flow through my mind, trying to make heads or tails of it all. If someone is out to hurt me, let them. If they are simply trying to scare me . . . well, it's working.

Sam's gone. Someone locked me in the attic. Could be a ghost; could be a serial killer, or maybe someone who just wants to torture me. I can't call the cops again because there's nothing they can do. Or they don't want to do it. Clearly, they think I'm making it all up; it's all in my head. They don't even believe anyone lives across the road!

I can't sit here anymore. My head is so full of what-ifs and everything that's been happening that I have to pace. I stand up and walk around a bit, then head to the porch. Stupid, I know. I should stay inside, where I'm probably safer. I go anyway.

I step into the dark porch and stand near the windows, staring across the road. There is still no sign of life. Where the hell is Sam? He went to check the barns because I told him I saw something. He's missing because of me. Who knows if I led him straight into danger? Sam would usually show up out of nowhere, but now he's vanished. Or maybe he just skipped town. I'm sure writers tend to be spontaneous like that, what with their ever-running creative minds. But without his car? Something in my gut is telling me that Sam didn't just get up and leave. There's something abnormal going on here.

What if what happened to Jeff happened to Sam?

That is an unexpected question in my head, and I immediately get frustrated as my thoughts start to spiral into a vortex of worst-case scenarios. *What if something* has *happened to Sam? What if he is hurt, lost, or worse?*

With a sudden burst of determination, I grab my sweater that's hanging behind me on the chair and slip it on. Enough of stewing in assumptions and speculations. I can't just sit idly by while Sam is missing. I have to do something—anything—to find him. If anything, it's partly my fault he's gone, and my ridiculous fear of the barns is what has kept me from properly searching for him in there. Plus, I'm no longer an eight-year-old kid. There's no boogeyman waiting to get me in the shadows. It's all in my head.

As I step outside into the cool night air, a sense of urgency washes over me. I'm going to search for Sam properly this time. *Really* search for him.

I head toward the barns, my flashlight cutting through the already forming darkness, a crescent moon in the sky as I arrive at the first large doors. With each step that I take to arrive here, the unease in my gut grows stronger, and a knot of dread tightens my chest.

Relax. There's no way I'll do a proper job of this if I'm already spooked.

"Sam! Sam!" The barn seems to swallow up my voice, barely giving off an echo.

If there are rats or bats in here, I wouldn't know it. There's no movement. Nothing responds. There's just the eerie silence of the countryside.

The interior is shrouded in darkness, the only illumination coming from the beam of my flashlight as it sweeps across the dusty floor.

Slowly, I venture further inside, my footsteps echoing in the empty space. There's nothing but the old machinery stored here and old mounds of hay. My anxiety mounts with each passing moment, and there is still no sign of Sam.

I walk to the far end of the barn now, aiming my light at every corner. Turning around, I notice the wooden ladder that leads to the loft, where my dad used to store more hay. I remember playing up there too.

"Sam! Are you up there?"

Silence. There's no way I'm going to climb up there; it's too risky. Yet, the gnawing thought that reminds me that I'll never be satisfied unless I check every inch of this place wins the war against my logic and I climb the ladder.

I'm halfway up, and I can see the bales of hay stacked up in one corner when my flashlight beam falls upon something unexpected—a flickering light dancing in the shadows.

My heart skips a beat, and I freeze. Someone's up there; there's freaking *light* coming from there! But I hear no sound. Slowly, I climb up the ladder and look around. There's nothing out of the ordinary. Except for the rusted lantern right in front of me, which is hosting a weak flame in the darkness.

What in the world?

I walk toward the lamp because I need to touch it; I need to know that I'm not hallucinating the damn old lamp! I don't even know why I'm mad as I march straight toward it, but when I touch the lamp, relief washes over me. It is quickly replaced by fear, though. Someone's staying here. I need to know who. *Or what.*

As if on cue, I catch sight of something moving in the shadows—a figure, tall and shadowy, whose form is hazy. It rises from the far end of the loft, like a genie, and I gasp, frozen in place. My eyes are yet to fully adjust to the darkness, but then the *thing* gives off a clicking sound. I've seen and heard enough to send me running back toward the ladder.

Shit, shit, shit, shit!

I try to scramble down the wooden ladder, but I see the *thing* coming toward me fast, and I fall to the ground. I land on my back, which completely knocks the air out of me.

My breath catches in my throat as I watch the shadow approaching, and I gasp, paralyzed with fear and pain, as the figure seems to materialize before my eyes.

It's a shifting shadow; that's the only way I can describe it. With a sudden burst of terror and adrenaline, I struggle to my feet, ignoring the sharp pain that erupts from my legs in protest, and turn to flee.

My head throbs, and as I push my way forward, I see the barn's entrance looming ahead, so I make for it with every ounce of energy I have left. But as I reach the door, I feel a cold hand close around my wrist, stopping me in my tracks.

That's when I start to scream.

I whirl around wildly in terror, ready to fight. My heart's pounding in my chest, but there is nothing there—only the empty darkness of the barn, silent and still as the grave.

"Oh my God, oh my God," I bawl out into the night,

tearing myself free from the phantom grip and stumbling out into the cool night air. I don't look back as I run away from the barn, my vision blurry from the tears that are streaming down my eyes.

It's real! My fears are real! The boogeyman is *coming to get me!*

I reach the safety of my house. It's laughable that I think I'm even safe. I shut the door and sink down to the ground, curling up into a ball, and cry until my whole body is spent and I don't have any more tears to spill.

There's something out there—something sinister lurking just beyond the edge of my perception, waiting patiently for me in the shadows. It probably already got Sam too.

CHAPTER 28

I DON'T KNOW what time it is or how long I've been sitting on the floor. I'm in a state of semiconsciousness, lost in a haze of sleepiness and wandering thoughts. My head feels like a boulder on my neck, and my right leg is tingling. It must have fallen asleep because of the way I was putting my weight on it. I slowly stand, shaking off the annoying tingling, and blink a few times. It's light out. It must be morning then. I wonder how long I was on the floor. Or *why* I was on the floor. What is happening to me?

Suddenly, there is a knock at the door, and my heart leaps into my throat. It's unlikely that a shadow creature would knock first before coming for me. Still, I hesitate for a moment before slowly rising to my feet. My legs are shaky beneath me. The knock comes again. It's presumptuous of me, I know, but my heart blooms with hope that maybe Sam's ok and he's by the door right now.

I swing the door open and find Megan standing on the doorstep instead. The moment she sees me, her expression turns to one of concern and worry.

"What are you doing here?" I ask, peeking around her to make sure she's alone. I'm still paranoid.

"Just wanted to stop in, say hi, see how you're doing."

I must look like a lunatic with my red-rimmed eyes and tousled hair. I run my fingers through my hair, breaking up a few tangles in the process.

"Megan, I need to know." I can hear my voice trembling as I speak, but I don't care. I'm done! Someone needs to tell me what is going on, or I might actually lose my mind here. "I need to know what happened when we were kids, why I left, everything. Please, Megan."

Megan looks hesitant, and I can see that she's uncertain. She has no idea how much of a last resort she is or how much I need her at this moment to just bring me out of the darkness I've been shrouded in for years.

"Melissa . . ." she begins but shakes her head. "Melissa, what's really going on? Did something happen?"

"Please, Megan, help me." The tears are threatening to come again, and I quickly swipe at my eyes, hating that she's seeing me like this in this state.

"Oh." Then, with a sigh, she finally nods. "Alright. Let's talk."

"Let me get us some coffee," I tell her as I walk to the stove to start a perk.

I set two mugs on the table. The strange doll is still there next to the salt and pepper shakers. I hadn't bothered it ever since it appeared there. It's another can of worms I've decided not to pry open. I was thinking that, at the right time, I'd remember the idea behind Kristi. I catch Megan eyeing the doll, but I don't explain. I should probably put it in a box or throw it away. But somehow, I haven't been able to do it.

"I'm ok. Just need to talk." That's the biggest understatement. I'm clearly *not* ok. "How are Rachel and the kids?" I'm trying to make small talk to calm down a bit before we talk about the elephant in the room.

"Oh, they're fine. The little one has started walking."

"Aww." I know nothing about kids, but picturing a little one toddling around unsteadily sounds cute.

I was just chased hours ago by a shadow, and I must look like something the cat threw up. Yet, somehow, the need to hold small talk before going to the main point is important to me.

When the coffee is finished, I pour two cups and hand one over to Megan before walking into the living room and sitting on the couch. She settles in next to me, and I wait, the silence stretching between us like a taut wire.

"What's going on, Melissa?" Megan says almost in a whisper. She takes a sip of her coffee and waits while I ponder the question.

"I had a rough night, that's all."

She nods but doesn't say anything. I'm not even sure where to start. I have so many questions. I know people in this town know something, and though I've been back and forth in my mind on whether or not to discover what happened in the past, I feel like last night sealed the decision for me. I must know.

"Why did I leave, Megan? What happened that made me disappear without a word?" I break our silence, taking a sip of the coffee I probably shouldn't be drinking due to my nerves.

Megan takes a deep breath, her eyes glistening in the soft light of the living room. "It's complicated, Melissa. There are things people just don't talk about because, well, we don't really know."

I reach out to place a hand on Megan's arm. "Please, Megan. I need to understand. I can't keep living in the dark, not knowing the truth."

She raises her eyebrows, and I have the feeling she is going to protest. Why in the world can't people just tell me? She must know more than she is letting on!

"Megan, things have been happening here. Strange things."

"Like what?" She lowers her mug, and I can see her hands trembling a little.

I proceed to tell her about things (people?) I've seen, the calls to the cops, getting locked in the attic. I don't tell her anything about Sam just yet. I'm not sure I will. It's bad enough that the look on her face tells me she probably things I'm looney anyway.

"I'm so sorry. I wish you would have let me know."

I laugh a little. "What could you have done?"

Megan sets her coffee on a nearby stand and sits back with a sigh. "I can't believe the cops didn't believe you."

"In their defense, they didn't find anything. Can't really blame them." *But I do.*

She sighs again. "Ok. Look. I'll tell you everything I know. Everything I heard. It's not a lot, though. And you have to promise me that you'll try to stay calm, no matter what I say."

I nod, wondering what she means. "I promise."

"Melissa, you and Jeff were inseparable as kids, like I

said. You were his best friend. You did everything together, even at school. I remember one time you tried to convince everyone else that you were siblings."

I lean into the softness of the couch, and the shadow of a smile lines my lips. I shut my eyes, letting the long-buried memories come back to me. Memories push through and float through my mind like a picture show. I remember the bond I shared with Jeff and the adventures we went on in the barns and the backyard.

"And then," Megan continues, her voice barely above a whisper, "that day at the silo . . . Jeff fell, Melissa. He fell, and everyone thought he was gone."

A chill sweeps through my veins at the mention of the silo.

CHAPTER 29

WE HEADED TOWARD the silo, hand in hand. I could feel Jeff trembling, and I wanted to call him names like "baby" and "chicken" but thought better of it. I was, after all, a little nervous myself. But, I reasoned, it was kind of thrilling to be doing something we weren't supposed to be doing. It wouldn't hurt . . . just to look inside.

We headed behind the barns to the silo that had trees surrounding it so we could get to the ladder from the branches, since the ladder was several feet off the ground, out of our reach.

Looking up at the tall concrete structure, I noticed it was bigger than I imagined it would be that close. The top was like a dome, and I wondered why it was shaped like that. Thin iron rungs served as a ladder, and there had to be about fifty of them. At the top was a ledge wide enough for two children to sit on, with rails around it.

We looked at each other, both with wide eyes. "Well?" I challenged, eyebrows raised.

Jeff nodded and gulped, then headed to the broken tree limb that led to the bottom run of the ladder. He jumped up to the first rung and began to climb. I carefully followed.

As we made our way up the ladder, we began to laugh. It is fun climbing up and being brave, *I thought to myself. I wondered what strange things were inside the silo and why my daddy never told me about them. They didn't look dangerous.*

We reached the ledge at the top. Jeff carefully climbed inside, as there was another ladder in the silo with the same ledge. I sat on the outer ledge and leaned over a little to peek inside. Far below was tons of grain. I saw birds flying around up toward the top, but that was it. Just birds and grain.

Looking at Jeff, I said, "Bor-ring! Just some dumb old grain."

"Melissa, it's so cool in here!" Jeff exclaimed excitedly, swinging his legs from the ladder. "Echo!!" His little voice echoed throughout the silo, and he laughed.

"Jeff, be careful," I warned, beginning to feel nervous. What if we fell? Would we sink into the grain? I didn't know anything about the grain in the silo. "We better get down before someone sees us."

"Just a few more minutes," Jeff begged. "Let's tell a story!"

"Ok, I guess . . ."

"So, once upon a time, there was a prince and princess, and they

climbed a tall tower!" Jeff began.

We loved the game of storytelling. We took turns and built stories together. Sometimes I would write our stories in my special notebook. I hoped to have it published someday and become a real author like Julie Campbell, who wrote Trixie Beldon books, or Carolyn Keene, who wrote Nancy Drew mysteries. I loved reading those old books.

"Your turn!" Jeff yelled, his little voice echoing in the semidarkness of the silo.

"And . . . they got to the top and saw a witch!" I exclaimed.

"The witch made the prince and princess scream," Jeff continued. "But then . . ."

"Then . . . the prince got brave and scared the witch off!"

We fell into a fit of giggles. That was fun, but my rearend was sore from sitting on the hard, cold ledge.

"Let's go, Jeff. Let's get a snack!"

"Ok," he agreed. "Mom made snickerdoodles. I bet we can have four each!" We loved the snickerdoodle cookies Jeff's mom made. "Start climbing down so I can reach that top rung."

I did as he told me, and when I looked up, I saw one of Jeff's small hands reaching out to the ledge. Suddenly, he let out a gasp.

My stomach churns with an overwhelming urge to vomit as I feel a searing heat creeping up my body while remembering this awful time so long ago. My head feels light and dizzy as if I'm about to pass out from the sheer intensity of it all. I take deep breaths and force myself to continue to remember.

"Jeff! Hold onto my hand!"

"I'm going to fall!" he screamed up at me, and he was crying.

We shouldn't have come here—to the silo. I didn't know what to do, and I was crying too. And those birds were there, circling above us. Their shadows played Ring Around the Rosie.

"Hold my hand; I'm going to pull you up!" I was on the ledge, leaning forward. Jeff was hanging . . . just hanging!

"But here's the thing, Melissa," Megan continues, oblivious to the revelation I'm having. My eyes are closed, and I start slowly rocking back and forth. "There were rumors and whispers that Jeff's family didn't want to let him go. That they refused to bury him and accept that he was truly gone. But the truth is, no one knew if he survived or not. People just assumed he died and made up the rumors."

Mommy and Daddy were arguing, and I could hear their voices from my room. I had only been out of my coma for a few days, but I knew what I was hearing.

"It was an accident! He fell."

"That is what you said the last time. Remember? She had an

accident, and now we don't have Marc anymore!"

"Shh, she'll hear you!"

"I can't look Shannon and Gary in the face anymore. They're not saying it, but they think she pushed him in. Everybody's thinking it. They all know what happened to Marc."

I felt tears come to my eyes. Shannon and Gary are Mommy and Daddy's friends—close friends. I felt bad thinking they may not be friends anymore. Because of me.

"And whose fault is that? Huh? You just had to tell Gary!"

"Oh my—"

My mind is reeling with the implications of what Megan is suggesting. *Could it be possible? Could Jeff still be alive after all these years?*

"I heard that the grief was too much for you and you had . . ." Megan's voice faded.

"What?"

"They said it made you lose your mind," she whispers.

Did they not know that I had fallen and had been in a coma?

"Soon after what happened to Jeff, your parents left. It happened so fast; one moment you were there, the next, you all moved away. Jeff's family moved too. People tried to talk to your grandma, but everyone was tight-lipped."

"But I came back at one point," I say softly. Megan

nods; she knows I came back briefly.

Suddenly, I have a crazy thought. "Maybe Jeff is alive." I can't believe I said that, but the thought popped into my head, and isn't it a possibility? I mean, no one had seen him but there hadn't been a funeral.

"Oh, um, remember, Melissa, they were rumors. No one ever saw Jeff again. They moved shortly after you guys did. Just upped and left in the middle of the night, no final goodbyes or anything."

Ahh. That would explain the stuff in the house across the road—boxes in the strange room, beds still made. Now I wish I had explored more thoroughly instead of just looking for Sam.

"But no one ever saw him get buried, right? You said it yourself."

"Well, no, but a lot of people assumed he died and the parents were too distraught to—"

"That doesn't make sense," I quickly cut in. "If he went to school around here, was my friend, and his parents knew my parents, surely there'd be a funeral or something. People don't just bury their kid and leave."

"I don't know," Megan hedged. She was pulling at an invisible thread on her shirt, not looking at me.

"None of this makes sense," I huff.

Megan looks up. "It doesn't. It never did. Some

believed he died and the parents quietly buried him to avoid hurting your family because whatever happened did so on their watch. Others believe he lived but was taken somewhere . . . well, you know. Away from here."

I sit there, my mind whirling. *Why doesn't anything make sense?* I lean over and place my head in my hands, willing my brain to come up with something that makes sense. Suddenly, I lift my head and look into Megan's eyes, my own widening.

"What are you thinking?" she asks warily.

"Sam!" I almost yell out. "Don't you see? Sam is Jeff!"

"Who? Your weird neighbor? No way."

"Yes! Oh, it all makes sense now! Remember when we saw him at the house? And he knew about Kristi! A complete stranger, knowing about my doll. What are the odds? And he was always calling me Lissy like he knew me."

Megan wasn't catching on; I could see it on her face. "Uh, who's Kristi?"

"The creepy doll!"

"What creepy doll . . .?" She pauses and takes a deep breath. "Look, we could just go ask him to be sure."

At that, I freeze. No, we can't, because Sam is missing. Vanished into thin air. Or fled. I still don't know the reason behind the bloody knife I found or the creepy things he wrote.

"I think he's gone on a trip or something. I haven't seen him in a while." That's all she needs to know. I don't need her thinking I'm crazy too.

Megan sips from her cup, looking thoughtful. "You know, if Sam truly is Jeff, and Jeff didn't die, maybe . . . Maybe he's not the person you once knew. Maybe he's out for revenge."

My mind races with the same thought. The memories of those typed papers in Sam's house flood back, my heart pounding with realization. *What if the woman he wrote about is me?* I can feel the sting of his callous words still, cutting deep into my soul. Sam—or is it Jeff?—must believe that I abandoned him when he needed me the most. But I didn't let him fall; I fought to save him! We were just innocent children, for goodness' sake! Something happened to me as well. It wasn't only Jeff who was hurt. Now, after all these years, here we are once again. Irony twists like a knife in my chest as I realize we are at the very place where it all happened.

Has he been the one messing with me all this time? I can't seem to relate the shadow creature in the barn to Sam because it still doesn't make sense. I saw it and felt its cold grip on my wrist.

Or maybe it was all in your head.

I hate this voice that keeps repeating this thing in my head. I know what I saw! Unless . . . No, that's a stretch. *But what if? What if it* is *Sam messing with me because he knows that I see things sometimes? It doesn't take much to bring monsters to reality; all you need is fear.*

It all makes sense now! Sam always appeared just at the right moment when I needed someone to save me. His reasons for being there were always too coincidental. "I needed to grab my mail." "I thought I heard a scream."

I've made up my mind. Sam is Jeff, and he is probably not missing. I'm now inclined to believe that he's waiting for the right moment to strike, perhaps when I'm unsuspecting.

"Yes," I finally say to Megan, distracted by my thoughts. "Maybe he *is* out for revenge."

"You need to be very careful, Melissa. You can come stay with me for a while to be safer."

I smile at her. That's the safest and most logical thing to do. It's been a while since I received genuine concern from someone, and it feels good knowing she is willing to keep me safe.

But this is between me and Jeff. It always has been. I need to face him on my own. No more running. No more being in the dark.

"I'll be alright."

"Are you sure?"

"Yes, yes. Trust me, Megan." I wave off her concern. "Thank you so much. For telling me all of it."

Something quickly flashes through Megan's eyes when I say that, but before I can read what it is, she smiles at me. "I'm just glad I could help you out."

We finish our coffee, and I walk Megan out the door.

"Be safe out here," she tells me before squeezing my arm.

"You too. Get home safe."

I wave goodbye and watch as her car leaves. Instinctively, I stare at Sam's house. I've been doing that a lot, nervous about his disappearance, but now that I know what I know, I'm convinced Sam is around. Probably looking at me right now.

I need to put it aside for now. I'm tired, and I need to try to sleep for a bit. I step back into my house and shut the door, wishing it had a lock.

* * * * *

"Jeff! Grab my hand, please!" I yelled.

"Lissy, help me!"

I felt desperate at his cries. What could I do? I watched as Jeff struggled to reach for my hand, my hand still holding onto the ladder rail. His eyes were wild with fear. I struggled to hold my footing on the ladder rung while holding on with one hand, the other holding my best friend.

"Melissa . . ."

I heard Jeff's frightened whisper. I yanked and pulled, but he was so heavy!!

"Jeff! Reach your other hand up; come on!"

"Melissa . . . help . . . me . . ."

"Jeff!"

There was pure fear in his eyes. Suddenly, his hand slipped from mine. I tried to grab it. Then I watched Jeff disappear into the darkness below.

"Lissy!"

I was kneeling on the ledge, leaning forward with my mouth wide open, a scream frozen on my lips. Then I pulled back before remembering I was so high up. And I fell.

I feel someone watching me even before I open my eyes. *Breathe in, breathe out.* My senses flare up, listening for anything. There's nothing to hear or smell; it's just the innate feeling that I'm being watched.

My eyes flutter open, and the chorus of birds outside explodes in my ears. I'm in bed, tangled up in my sheets. I had a dream, but I can't remember what it was about.

I let myself enjoy the moment, chasing away the

foreboding I felt seconds ago. Maybe I'm paranoid, maybe I'm right, but if Sam is creeping around in my house, that's his business. I'm exhausted from being jumpy, and all I want to do is leave. There's only one thing left to do, and that is to talk to Sam. Jeff.

Sighing, I get up from the bed and straighten up the sheets. I grab some clean clothes, deciding I need a shower to soothe away the nightmares. I'm not sure what my plan is after that. Part of me says NO COFFEE because basically my nerves are shot. The last thing I need is caffeine. I would like to keep my wits about me, so maybe I'll just drink a lot of water today.

Suddenly, I get that feeling again that I'm being watched. I turn to face the door, which is slightly ajar, and catch a glimpse of a shadow on the wall just outside the door in my bedroom. I freeze, waiting. It stays for a few seconds, and then it moves away. I can't move from my spot. I don't dare. I don't hear footsteps, but the shadow moved. What in the world is going on!

After a few seconds, I tiptoe to the door and kick my foot through the opening. If someone is out there, they'll probably grab my leg thinking it's my entire body coming out since it's happening so fast. But no one grabs my leg. I slowly stick my head out, and to my relief, the hallway is empty.

I step back into my room and walk over to the window looking out at the backyard. I see a few birds flying around, and a squirrel darts across the lawn. My eyes roam over the barns and land on the tallest silo. Then, for some reason, my heart slams in my chest.

CHAPTER 30

THE SILO. THAT'S where it all began.

After I calmed down after my near panic attack this morning, I went on with my day and actually felt pretty calm for some reason. Maybe because things have become clear; the puzzle pieces put together.

Now it's evening, and the sun is dipping below the horizon, casting long shadows across the farmstead.

Standing in the fading light, my gaze fixes on the silhouette of the silo looming in the distance. Naturally, I feel unease prickle at the back of my mind just looking at it, but thankfully, I don't get a panic attack. I know that I must visit the silo one more time. I'm not sure what pulls me there or how I know that I need to walk over to the silo at that moment, but I start to walk across the uneven ground.

My bare feet sink into the soft earth with each stride, and the air is heavy with the scent of rain mixed with dust and old hay. As I approach the silo, my heart quickens. It's like I'm anticipating something, but I'm not sure what it is. I'm not supposed to be near the silos.

But here I am . . .

My gaze is drawn upwards to the towering silo, and I am overcome with a sudden wave of crushing grief. It feels like a heavy weight has settled on my heart, stealing the breath from my lungs. My eyes sting with unshed tears as I realize that I have never truly mourned. Yes, I was unconscious right after the accident, but even then, it's as if my mind quickly sealed away the horror of it all, preventing me from grieving for my friend or remembering him at all but for some fleeting memories. I never had the chance to properly say goodbye or mourn his loss. If, in fact, he truly is gone. And now, standing in front of this silent reminder of what happened, those suppressed emotions come rushing back to the surface and threaten to consume me once more.

It had been an accident, that's all. Just an accident . . .

"That you caused. You're always one to cause accidents, aren't you?"

I know better than to look around and try to find the voice speaking to me. It's only me. These are my thoughts, and I think they are out loud in the real world, but they aren't.

Jeff may have fallen. But I think he's alive.

I swipe at my eyes, then take a deep breath to settle the emotions. Reaching out, I grasp the rusted rung of the ladder that leads up into the silo. My fingers curl tightly around the cold metal for a few seconds before I heft myself up and begin to climb.

Something howls in the distance—maybe a dog or a wolf. As I ascend higher and higher, the sky becomes clearer to me. I can't see the moon tonight; the sky is just a black sheet dotted by tiny sparkling stars. Each step I take flashes a memory of that day, of eight-year-old me climbing up the ladder. One step, and it's my bare foot. Another step is my tiny foot in my running shoes.

Finally, I reach the top of the silo, and my breath comes in ragged gasps. I'm wearing a T-shirt and jeans despite the chill in the air. Bare feet because . . . well, I didn't think to put them on in my state of mind.

I stand there for a moment and let my eyes scan the horizon then back to the silo. There's nothing extraordinary about this contraption. I can't believe we were so obsessed with it when we were younger, Jeff and me. And look what happened.

I sit on the ledge in front of the gaping hole of the silo. Something rustles inside, and I still. Suddenly, a bird bursts out, and I jump so quickly I almost lose my grip and slip.

"Shit!"

I grip the rail, willing myself not to look down. My heart is racing wildly, and everything in me is telling me that this is a terrible idea. Sitting at the top of the silo where it all began. The laughter, the stories . . . the accident. *Was it an accident?* Of course it was. I scold myself for thinking that it never was. Of course I tried to save Jeff. He was my best friend.

I hear footsteps climbing up the metal rung, approaching from below me, the sound echoing in the stillness of the night. I don't look down; I don't need to. I already know who it is.

"Hello, Jeff," I say softly, my voice barely above a whisper.

He doesn't answer. I hadn't expected him to. I still don't look. I don't care if he has a weapon; I just want this to end.

"Why did you come back?" I ask, facing the silo. *This damn silo. Why did we ever come up here in the first place? Oh, yeah. I dared him.*

"You let me die," he whispers.

"You *didn't* die," I whisper back.

He doesn't speak for a minute, and then he comes up closer to me. I can feel him—his presence so strong though he's right below me. So close. After all these years. Here we are again. We're back to the beginning. A boy and a girl on a silo they know better than to be on. The whole earth is still, and it spreads through the air like a thick fog. Even though there's no moonlight, the rusted metal of the silo glows against the darkness.

"You left me to die. You could have saved me if you tried harder."

I don't respond because I know he's being irrational. And he clearly is insane. I wait.

"It was one of your father's farmhands who pulled me out, you know." I didn't know. I didn't know anything about this. He gives a small laugh. "I managed to scream before I went under. I was pulled out but unconscious."

I open my mouth to say something, but he moves. It's a small motion, and the ancient metal creaks beneath our weight. Maybe it will give way and devour us both in the darkness.

My entire body tenses as I look down and study him. The tension between us thickens, and there are so many emotions going through me right now, I can barely keep my focus. This is Jeff. *My* Jeff. My childhood best friend.

Supposedly dead, caused by my dare. But Jeff, pretending to be someone else, to scare me . . . torment me? Get revenge? It can't be possible. I'm so confused. I can barely breathe through all the emotions.

A gust of wind rushes against me, and I ignore the shivers that courses through my body. Jeff creeps closer and stands before me where I sit. He's gripping the rail with one hand, the other hand in his pocket, his feet planted on a rung. So casual. Our silence is becoming louder, and I finally cast a wary glance at Jeff, who is staring in my direction. His expression is unreadable, and his gaze is fixed on the yawning mouth of the silo. I don't need a mind reader to know what he's thinking.

"Melissa, you were my best friend. You let me down. You dared me to go up there. I fell. You . . . didn't save me. I almost died."

That's when I look him in the eyes. Jeff. Those dark eyes. I stare at him, studying his face, though it's not easy, given it is nighttime. But it's recognizable now. I didn't see it before because I couldn't remember who he was. But now . . . Memories come rushing back. I almost smile, despite myself. My best friend. Like a brother to me. I feel tears seeping into my eyes, and I look down, unable to meet his eyes anymore.

"I'm sorry. I tried. I did everything I could. I reached for you. I was so little! I couldn't hang on; I just couldn't." There is a pleading tone in my voice. I am helpless to stop it. "I *reached* for you. Then I slipped, and I must have hit my head. I fell too."

"You survived."

"So did you!" I cry as I whip my head up to look at him again. "You're *here*! Why do you want revenge? Why do you hate me?"

His lips form a grin that looks so . . . evil. Angry. "I was in the hospital for months. I had many surgeries. Doctors said I'd never be one hundred percent better. My brain—"

"But you're fine!" I insist. "You're a writer. You live here. You're fine."

"No, Melissa. I'm not." He stares at me for a minute before his eyes narrow. He's so close to me, I can feel his breath. "I'm not a writer. I made that up. Growing up, I went through so much physical and mental therapy. I could barely do anything on my own until I was in my early twenties. I'm not even supposed to drive a car. I suffered from that fall—nearly drowning and suffocating in that damned grain. And it's all your fault."

"But . . ." I'm practically pleading at this point. "You have been pretending to be someone else. Sam. I mean, if you're really Jeff . . ." His sudden wicked smile does not escape my notice. "We can talk this out. We were best friends!"

He laughs now. "Exactly. We *were.* That ship has sailed. My parents had to move because of what happened."

Deep breaths. I must remember to breathe. *Keep talking and distract him.*

"Ok," I say slowly. "That was many years ago. Maybe we can get therapy together! Work things out. I know if you just talk to me, you'll—"

"I will never forgive you. You killed your brother, then you tried to kill me."

I gasp at his words. *I killed my brother? No! No, no, no! It's not true.* I never had a brother! I shake my head, but he's not breaking eye contact and is moving closer to me.

"Everything I do is monitored in my life in case I can't handle it. Therapy. Check-ins. You don't know what that's like!" He is almost shouting now, and I start to tremble. "This affected my brain! I will never be completely normal like everyone else. All because of you!"

Realizing how much danger I'm in up here, I glance around, looking for an escape. This man is crazy. *Is he really even Jeff? Maybe he's some lunatic pretending to be Jeff!* No. His eyes. *This is Jeff. Right?* I look down, thinking of making a leap for it, but that would surely lead to my demise.

Jeff—Sam?—suddenly leans closer to me, and my heart feels like it's going to beat out of my chest. He's so close, and he's blocking the way down. I can't escape. The only way I can go is . . . well, through the mouth of this blasted contraption! But I'll die if I do! Even if there was soft grain, I'd die.

I do my best to focus on this man before me, waiting for him to lunge. This can't be Jeff; that sweet boy died—or didn't—when he fell in the silo. My best friend. Like a brother.

No, it can't be. This is Sam. I'm convinced of that now. My Jeff would never ever want to hurt me. He always forgave me. This is definitely Sam. And he wants to kill me. I had totally gotten it wrong before. My thinking had been muddled. Yes, this is Sam.

"Sam! Listen to me!"

"Don't call me that!" He spits it out at me, his eyes darkening. "You know I'm Jeff. Sam doesn't exist."

Tears fill my eyes, but I do my best to hold them back. I have to keep my composure if I want to live.

"You have no idea how long I've waited for this moment. For you to feel how I felt. To *die*."

The venom in his voice turns my blood cold. I'm crying now, despite myself, and I know that this is a day that might take my life. I've always wanted to know what happened, and now I do. The realization that this is truly Jeff shatters my heart.

Suddenly, with a malevolent sneer, he lunges at me, a crazed glint in his eyes. I let out a blood-curdling scream, desperately clinging onto the rungs of the ladder as he tries to pry my grip away. My heart pounds with fear as we teeter on the edge of the silo, inches away from its gaping mouth.

"Please don't do this!"

He chuckles darkly, his voice dripping with venom and hate. "You are powerless now. Older, but stupid!"

I try to reason with him, begging for us to stop this madness before something terrible happens to one of us. But his hate-filled eyes only grow more menacing.

"We don't have to do this, Jeff," I plead again and again as he ignores my desperate cries.

"Oh yes we do, *Lissy*."

With that final declaration, he lunges at me again, and I quickly move out of the way, barely managing to hold on to the edge of the ladder. Suddenly, without any warning or hesitation, he goes flying into the silo, dangling off its decrepit edge for a brief moment before tumbling below.

I glance over my shoulder in shock at the sight before me. The absolute surprise and terror frozen on his face. It's a moment that will stay with me forever.

CHAPTER 31

THE NURSE CHECKS the young woman's vitals, dims the lights, and makes sure the classical music is still playing on the CD player the woman's parents had left for her. Such nice people, the woman's parents. Nurse Alma shakes her head sadly at the thought. *Such nice people, holding onto their daughter's life when they know she's never coming back to them. Not fully anyway.*

"All set, dear Melissa. Sleep tight," Nurse Alma whispers to the patient. She's so young, this girl, and it saddens the nurse so much that she's in this sorry state. Life can be cruel when it wants to be.

As she steps out of the room and pulls the door shut, a

man with dark hair and mysterious dark eyes approaches. He is holding a clipboard.

Alma waits until he comes to a stop in front of her. "Can I help you?" she whispers. No one can hear her, but she always likes to think that it's respectful to whisper regardless. She has never seen this man in the facility, let alone on this unit.

"Sorry to be stopping by so late," the man says in a low voice, and she smiles approvingly at his tone. "I'm Dr. Pierce. I'm here to . . ." He looks at the papers on his clipboard before continuing. "I'm here to check on Melissa Stevens."

"Oh. This is her room. Are you her new doctor?"

"I am."

Nurse Alma and the new doctor stand in the hallway for a few minutes, assessing each other. She had been told earlier that there would be a new doctor who'd be taking over Melissa's *situation.* Alma didn't like the idea of letting all these doctors in, just to treat her patients like lab rats.

The facility is quiet at this time of night. The patients are asleep, and the nurses have finished their rounds. Alma always takes special care of Melissa, though. She isn't sure why. Maybe she feels about what happened or the fact that she was in a coma and now not well enough to get out. Such a troubled life at such a young age, and now as an adult, stuck in a facility for the rest of her life.

"Ok," she says slowly. "She's sleeping now. Best to leave her that way."

"Can you tell me a little more about her?" the doctor asks with a glint of interest in his eyes.

Alma is about to protest, but the doctor looks so sincere. It is late and quite unorthodox to give a patient rundown to a doctor in a hallway at night, but she can give him some information on her patient. His new patient.

"Well, when she came out of her coma, she was not the same. She lashed out, spoke incoherently, and had no idea where she was most of the time. Poor girl kept thinking she returned to the farmhouse where the, um, accident happened when she was just a young girl."

"Did she return?" he asked.

"She did. Not for long, though. She ended up leaving again. Her parents couldn't handle her. It was traumatic for her, but no one understood." Alma shakes her head at the thought. Such a sweet, troubled girl. A girl who told Alma stories about the farm where she had lived. And stories they were, because the poor dear can't remember much of her childhood.

The doctor clears his throat, and Alma continues. "We keep her sedated a lot. Safety reasons, you understand?"

"I understand," the young doctor comments with a sad look on his face, which Alma approves of. Perhaps here's another sympathetic doctor who genuinely cares about the patients—not like the rest. "And her parents?"

Alma wonders why he is asking so many questions, especially at this hour. But she decides it will be better to answer him now, so on her next shift she can get back to work and not be bothered.

"Oh, well they visit once a month. It's too hard on the mother, you see, to see her daughter in this state. And she doesn't seem to be getting better . . ." Alma trails off and glances around almost nervously.

"So she's been here this entire time, eh?" The doctor glances at the door, looking curious now.

"Well, she was living in a home for people with . . . well, certain needs. She couldn't completely be on her own even though she's an adult. But she only lasted there, oh, say six or seven months. Her episodes increased and doctors decided she needed to be in a permanent care home. So her parents keep her here for safety and in hopes she'll recover some day. She gets therapy, but it doesn't seem to help."

"And she thinks she leaves and returns home, is that it?"

"Yes. So sad. In fact, today she had another one of her

dreams. She went back to the farm where she lived before the accident. She keeps insisting she's returned and that someone . . . Well, I've said enough."

The doctor looks intrigued, but Alma won't finish. She's said her piece—too much, if she's being honest with herself—and the doctor can look at Melissa's chart if he wants further information.

"Anyway, I've grown close to her through the years. She trusts me most, I imagine." The doctor only nods, still looking at the door. "Well, my shift is over. You're welcome to check on the patient, but please don't talk to her. Don't mention . . . the silo."

The doctor turns to her and smiles. "No worries, Nurse. I'll take good care of our . . . patient."

Alma smiles and nods once, then proceeds down the hallway. It is late, and she has to get home. She is exhausted and looking forward to having some of that leftover stew her husband made for dinner.

The young doctor walks into the room and over to the sleeping patient. He stares at her sleeping face for a long while before taking her hand in his.

"Melissa," he whispers, caressing her hand with a thumb.

The young woman opens her eyes, feeling quite groggy. She figures she was probably given medication, like always.

She squints up at the figure looming over her, feeling confused, then she startles. *Who is this? What is he doing in my room? A doctor?* But he looks like someone she knows . . .

"Who . . ." she starts to say, but her tongue feels like cotton. Where is Nurse Alma? The one who mothers her and takes such good care of her?

"You let me down," the man leaning over her whispers. "You literally let me down. But I didn't die. No, I didn't die, and I am here to give you what you deserve."

"But . . ." She struggles to sit up, but her head feels so heavy. Her heart is racing, and her breathing has become labored.

"You were my best friend once upon a time. But you left me for dead. And now it's time you paid."

What is he talking about? She's trying to make sense of it all, but her head is so groggy. She then notices that he's holding something. It almost looks like a syringe. She is familiar with those, with all the medications she gets daily. Now, she's frozen with fear, unable to scream or move.

He leans over and whispers, "You can't get rid of me that easily."

She opens her mouth to scream . . .

If you enjoyed this book, please consider taking a few minutes to leave a *positive* review on Amazon and Goodreads!

Thanks for reading! I hope you enjoyed *The Silo*. I had come up with the title before I knew the book's topic. One day, while driving to the farmhouse to visit my grandma, I happened to look over at the barns. The idea struck me when I saw the silo—the sun lowering behind it and casting creepy shadows around it.

I grew up living in the country on my grandparents' farm with them, my mom, sister, and uncle. We had amazing neighbors—Duane, Debbie, Marc, Kristi, and Jeff—and many memories on Shells Bush Road.

As kids, we often played in the barns, but we were told not to go in the silos. I knew why, of course. I was aware of the dangers when the silos were full.

Melanie Lopata is a published author of children's books and adult fiction who resides in upstate New York with her husband and her beloved pets. She is the CEO of a publishing company called Get It Write Publishing Company (www.getitwritepublishing.company) and a professional editor. When not working or writing, Melanie enjoys reading (psychological thrillers are her favorites!), taking walks, and spending time with friends, family, and her pets.

Visit her blog, Beyond Publishing, at www.beyondpublishing.blog

For more books by this author, visit www.MelanieLynnCollection.com

Made in the USA
Columbia, SC
11 October 2024